Shaadi -ka- Laddoo .Com

Chuckling encounters in search of a suitable groom!

NAVNIIT GANDHI
VARUNA KHULLAR

Readomania

Readomania Publishing
A division of Kurious Kind Media Private Limited
908, Vishwadeep Building, District Centre, Janakpuri,
New Delhi – 110058
books.readomania.com
email: contact@readomania.com
Facebook: facebook.com/iamreadomania
Twitter: twitter.com/iamreadomania
Instagram: iamreadomania

First Published in 2019 by Readomania

ISBN: 978-93-85854-85-9

Typeset in Palatino Linotype by Shine Graphics
Printed at Thomson Press (India) Ltd.

Readomania

India has traditionally been the land of storytellers and a lot of us have an inherent skill of creating good plots, good stories and good narrations. With a little encouragement and support, many more authors will be widely read and attain a place in the sun. This is the essence of *Readomania*—an initiative that nurtures emerging stars of the literary world.

It would not be an exaggeration to say that *Readomania* is the talent hunt in fiction. It goes a step beyond by not just identifying the talent but also nurturing it and showcasing it to the world. In the process, we have created a powerhouse of content.

Readomania has four principal interest areas—traditional print publishing, online library of short stories and poetry, literary events and products.

The print publishing works towards delivering good quality content to the readers. We publish good authors in meaningful anthologies, novels and works of narrative non-fiction. Our books stand out for their perspectives, the plots, the language and most importantly their ability to enrich lives.

Take a break, read something nice, write something beautiful. Read our books or visit us at www.readomania.com and enjoy a whole new world of literature.

'A fantastic read! I ended up meeting quite a few of my college friends in the characters. It expertly presents the dilemma of a modern woman stuck between parental pressure, societal pressure and her own aspirations. Many observations and stories are sewn up with a great balance of humour and bitter truths!'

—Amit Tandon, *Stand-Up Comedian*

'What an amazing book! It made me laugh and chuckle all the way. The story is so relatable; the characters are so very believable and honest that every reader shall laugh out loud and recollect the proposals brought to us and those whom we rejected on silly grounds; and the pre-conditions we had set while looking for the perfect match, in total disregard of our own flaws! I felt I was looking into a mirror... Ha! Ha! Ha!'

—Ssumier Pasricha a.k.a. *Pammi Aunty*

To,

All the MOMS…who persuade, push, pester and prevail upon their sons and daughters to marry.

Without you, dear Moms, there would be no GenNext!

A Few Words

Girls and boys in India grow up with dreams in their eyes; dreams that have largely been planted there by their mothers. If there is one challenge every Mom desperately runs after in an attempt to catch it by the neck and bring it into her living room, embrace it, and then pats herself for the coup—it is that of finding and seizing the perfect spouse for her children! She pursues the challenge—unfettered and undaunted, innocently believing that her own ward being the 'bestest', deserves the most eligible and perfect groom or bride (as may be available).

Almost everybody marries in India. Well, men and women marry all over the world, but their marriages are no match for ours... Ours are all about fun, masti, relatives, gifts, glitz and good food, while theirs are solemn affairs minus any brouhaha! Moreover, the roles that enthused Moms in India play in arranging the weddings of their darlings is by no means a feat possible for mothers elsewhere to accomplish.

It is to assist the doting and warrior-type mothers who are otherwise also sufficiently braced up for the challenge, that the tech-geeks unassumingly brought the magic of the 'www.com' at our doorstep. Numerous online portals have mushroomed and added spice and variety to the hitherto a-little-dull process of match-making.

The scope of the search for the most perfect, alias—the most beautiful/handsome, slim/well-built, tall, fair, loving, independent, gracious, well-educated, polite, professionally well-established with brighter horizons and one who believes in traditional values but is equipped with a modern outlook and belongs to an illustrious and humble family girl/boy—has indeed become wider and substantial.

Hurray!

Go, Moms, go… The challenge is all yours! The online matrimonial portals are yours to use in your gallantry missions! Grab the challenge with both hands, for your grip shall now be firmer too!

Come on,

Click!

The Chuckles

It was a fine day with the sky bright and blue when I left college that day. Clearly, I had not anticipated the *blah-blah…boo-hoo…boooosh* awaiting me at home.

As I entered the living room, Mom's opening lines were:

'Do you realise that you are not getting any younger? You are 37 years old, for goodness sake! What have I done to deserve this? Why must I listen to all the scathing remarks thrown at me by the whole world? Oh God, when will you listen to my prayers? Did I do anything awful to deserve this?'

Before you wonder what I did to invite such melodrama, the reference was to my single status, and the resultant heartburns it was giving to the whole wide world outside.

It is not that I have always been *single.* My status was indeed '*married*' for a few years, until it changed to '*divorcee*', about four years ago. When it was *single* till the age of 30, people kind of sympathised with me. There simmered a dash of hope in their eyes about me. After the divorce, I had innocently presumed that I would be *single* once again. Technically, I was, but I was mercilessly robbed of the comfort zone that came with the *single* status. At first, a few accusing glances were shot at me, and then a few murmurs about why the marriage must have not lasted and then the piteous looks followed and stayed. *Poor girl, there is a full life ahead and she is a divorcee now*—dozens of eyes seem to be saying that.

A set of three loving family members; a steady and valued job at a college; and my happy-go-lucky temperament seemed to be of no consequence to the 'well-meaning' Aunts and Uncles in the family and neighbourhood. *Did they pity themselves? Could it be that my happy status was a bit too much for the inconsolably married souls?* Anyhow, the comfort zone I had (despite the *looks*) managed to create for myself was being snatched from me bit by bit since months.

In fact, I had seen it all coming... Over the past few months, Mom and Papa had been at the receiving end of some stern looks of accusation and something to the effect of *how-can-you-sit-with-ease* when a divorced daughter in her late thirties is sitting at home. Soon, Mom started murmuring words of discontent regarding my present status. The nudging, at first, was mild and directed more at Papa. Then, the intensity of her words and emotions became stronger, the sighs louder and the sarcasm sharper!

That day, when my visibly-upset Mom started it all over again, my mind was working on the frailties of her nervous system and the math of it all. Probably something to do with a nerve which kept getting over-stimulated every fourth or fifth morning with frustrating regularity? And the stimulated nerve ballooned to its zenith by mid-afternoon, and unless a big fat verbal dose came pouring out, uninterruptedly, for about 30 minutes—the nerve simply threatened to burst. Wary of the grave consequences which would ensue if the bubbles of anxiety were capped inside, we wretched souls (three of us, excluding Mom) listened to the regular outbursts in nervous silence. Our heads were usually bent low during such solemn episodes. Solemn, yes...but, only when Papa, my younger brother Shaurya and I—the glum souls, allowed it to remain a monologue.

On those rare days, when any one of us chose to reply or to present counter-arguments—the scene at home became a war-zone. We, the warriors, were soon wounded...dashed to the ground and within less than an hour, ambushed! Words, bold declarations, scathing comments, anguished remarks and sighs of resignation flew high and all-around.

The above scenes were often catalysed by any boastful invitation card announcing the wedding of a younger cousin or of a younger girl or boy in the neighbourhood. *Why did these giggling girls and half-witted boys announce their weddings with such pomp and gaiety?*

The hubbub usually started when one of those nosy aunts who loved to rub salt on wounds, dropped in to say a harmless '*hello*'. By the way, even a scene in one of the soap operas on television sometimes sufficed in igniting the fireworks! Any of the above triggers usually occurred just before the onset of a weekend and our plans to spend it cosily tucked in warm blankets, were dashed.

On that day, Mom was rambling on, and I was wondering who the villain was this time? Was it another wedding card? Or, a casual visit by an Aunty? There was a brief interruption, when Papa—unaware that the big fat and too-familiar oration had started—meekly popped in the kitchen and reluctantly asked Mom if it was possible to have pakoras with chai? Poor Papa! He was caught in the crossfire. Mom gave him an accusing glance and roped him in, without much ado.

'How can you be so cool? I must say that something is either seriously wrong with all of you or probably I am the only sensitive one here... No, there will be no pakoras made in the house, until Binnie is married. With all these fried savouries, she will put on weight and all the curves will make her look older than ever. As it is, the lines on her face are giving me sleepless nights....'

Papa had become a wise old man over the years. Mom's verbal outbursts had given him an uncanny ability to either foresee when an outburst was on its way or if he did miss on that, he had mastered the art of wriggling out of the firing range, unscathed. He did the latter very smoothly at that minute. I was still taking a lot of time and had not acquired Papa's skills.

Mom was in no mood to relent easily. The spotlight fell on me, once again.

'Binnie, is there no mortal on this Earth who shall fit the bill? Why are you so stubborn? Why can you not compromise and settle for someone who is a normal man? Oh God! With the long list of expectations you are carrying in your head, how are we ever going to find that superman?'

And then, the final blow fell!

'Pummy Aunty is also much worried on your account. Yesterday, she came and gave a sensible idea. She suggested that we ought to register you on *shaadi-ka-laddoo.com*. Well, it has given me a lot of hope… We will have wider choices now.'

I protested at this fresh salvo and told her in no uncertain words that I was not going to trust proposals from the virtual world. At first, I tried to reason calmly, but Mom was on another plane altogether. I had to fume and fret and stomp my feet and bang the door while I walked out of the kitchen. All of it was in vain, though.

'Binnie, Pummy Aunty and I have already registered you on the matrimonial site. If you don't have an iota of sensitivity left in you so as to understand my woes, it is fine! I will check the proposals and filter them out for you... Hope you will show some decency and engage in polite conversations with those whose numbers and details I will be sending you. We are not your enemies here. Look at your age! Who do you think will take care of you when we are gone? Can I expect you to be at least a little considerate towards your aging and worried parents?'

A grim scene suddenly flashed before my eyes: *An 85-year-old me—teary-eyed and alone in a large house, suffering inconsolably from an undiagnosed disease and trying to lift a glass of water... And, crrrrrraccccc...the glass falls down.*

I felt a chill down my spine. I looked expectantly at Papa, quietly urging him to take over. He shot a pleading look back, and then winked at me with a smile.

I managed a small, a very small smile in return.

Mom came out of the kitchen with a plate full of cookies that she had baked in the morning and placed it before Papa. There was relief in her demeanour.

Perhaps, she too had been anxious about my reaction to being registered on the site. The weight seemed to have lifted off her chest. With a look of resignation, I picked up a cookie.

'Binnie, would you like to see the photograph of yours which we have uploaded on the site? It is the one in that short, beige-coloured skirt with a navy-blue cardigan—the one that you wore while you were in Bhutan in January this year,' Mom added with a chuckle.

The cookie crumbled—a little in my mouth and a little on the lap.

The First Laddoo

It was now all out in the open. The shift had occurred. From a few off-hand feeble attempts here and there by this Uncle or that Aunty, I was now formally perched on a matrimony platform. My status had a new little addition: Single< Married< Divorced< Single< On-the-Look-Out-Again.

Mom was aware that there were few avenues in my life to find that special someone on my own. I teach in a college—which means that either there are the old, grey-haired professors all around me or the nincompoop youngsters. *Not the most potential place to meet my dream man*. Furthermore, I am neither a party hopper, nor a shopper. I have a history of failed attempts at mingling in the singles' clubs, trek meets and at other networking events.

No wonder then that Pummy Aunty and Mom had zeroed down on a popular online matrimonial platform which they believed was a one-stop solution for my needs and their worries. After all, as Mom kept excitedly putting it across to Papa: *Where else are we going to get this kind of variety and diversity in terms of cities and countries, language, complexion, hobbies, titles, and appearances? Everything under one roof! You just wait and watch… Our Binnie is going to get the best one out there.*

For the next week or two, Mom was bubbling with cheer—basking at the prospect of sitting in the luxury of one's living room and scrutinising proposals (one after the other) that would tumble out of the laptop screen.

Shaadi-ka-laddoo.com offered a wide range of choice in terms of membership:

- ✓ Free (Only Profiles)
- ✓ Silver (Profiles + Chats + Emails)
- ✓ Gold (More Profiles + Chats + Emails + Pestering Customer Care Calls)
- ✓ Platinum category (More & more Profiles + Chats + Emails + Pestering and more pestering customer care calls)

Guided by the able advice of Pummy Aunty, Mom had settled for the Silver package, so she told me.

'Binnie, let me tell you… I honestly do not think you are made up of stuff that can survive in a typically Indian household setting. I have therefore stated a preference for guys settled abroad,' she declared.

I chose not to react at that statement. I wondered whether the statement was a compliment that I am way too above the trivia that dominates families here or was it meant to chide me for being far too free-spirited.

The first *laddoo*: Sri Ranganathan

After months of sieving, rejecting, and pretending to be considering—Mom paused at the profile of one Mr Sri Ranganathan.

Height: 5'8"; Complexion: Dark; Built: Medium (77 kg); Residence: Hampshire, London (own house); Religion: Hinduism (Tam Bram); Marital Status: Divorced (once); Issues: None; Family: Lost my parents a few years ago. One sister lives in Chennai with her husband and son.

Mom carefully calculated the pros: Aha! Looks intellectual: half-bald and glasses; settled in London; holds a British passport; has a PG degree in Economics and Public Policy; has an attention-worthy corporate title; is a sky diver and book lover; doesn't have children, and believes in gender-equality! Perfffecctt!

And then reluctantly, she weighed the obvious cons: South Indian and a little dark in complexion... Obviously, a big con for a North Indian mother!

Brushing aside her own reservations as silly idiosyncrasies, she sternly instructed me to accept the invitation to connect.

'Binnie, you will only have one sister-in-law to worry about if need be. Imagine, a life with no parents-in-law! I have no issues with parents but just that life will be easier for you considering how unsocial you are. Now, don't just stare at me. Accept your first match with grace.'

I hit the 'accept' button. The response was instant.

Scene 1: The beginning.

I take a close look at his profile. *Oh, wow!* In addition to the pros Mom had listed, I notice a few more: he was a winner at a popular game show in the UK, he stayed alone and loved to travel (Hmm...), was briefly married and is clear about what he wants from life.

All righty, Sri Ranganathan*ji*! *Wannakam*!

We exchanged *introductions* on the chat-wall. And for the next three days, we sent to and fro formal messages about who we were and what we did and what we liked, etc. I was amazed at how I had got over my initial (and stubborn) resistance to chatting with strangers against a virtual backdrop.

One day…

Sri: 'Hey Leena! Let's do a video call.'

Me: 'Hey Sri, I am game, when?'

And then, lo! There was a long talk, followed by longer chats and then many more video calls. We discussed nearly everything which two people inhabiting different terrains and nations find it very convenient to discuss, *errr—compare,* such as the weather, the people, the traffic, the cleanliness, the courteous *versus* the cheeky people, and the food options available. After our chats took off, I realised that such long-distance dating or affairs or marriages carried immense benefits: one could go on for days comparing silly things, without ever having to talk as much as an iota of sense! And life could thus very smoothly sail....

After days (Mom's glaring eyes notwithstanding) of such comparative analyses, I asked myself: *Is this going to lead somewhere? Let's see... It does seem to be going smooth!*

Scene 2: Cut to the second month!

Sri shares that he is done with the unreliable status of life in a foreign land and the unpredictability of the future. He said that he planned to move back to India. He had dreams, he said. To be particular, dreams of starting four start-ups! Yes, at one go!

Meanwhile, Mom's comments were getting spicier by the day: 'What are you both up to? Just talking for hours and hours? Why don't you decide soon? Who takes this much time, pondering over this and that? We never did... And see, we have lived happily since then! I have already begun to read about the customs of these South Indians at the time of marriage. By the way, you don't have to look extra fair in front of him... What if he gets a complex?'

Scene 3: The third month.

Sri takes a break from the Brits and lands in Hyderabad—trying to launch four start-ups at the same time. He has not started complaining exactly but he, more than often, lets me know of the efforts he is taking to adjust to the heat and traffic in India, all the while trying to chat regularly with his dear Leena. (*Ah, yes…that is me!)*

Chat 150th:

Me: 'Let's meet if you are serious about settling down.'

Sri: 'Yes, let's meet. And, the right time is now! The start-ups could start any time.'

Scene 4: The fifth month.

Sri and I decide to meet in Bengaluru where I was to attend a training program. Though Mom had raised a ruckus at home—which sounded thus: *Have you ever heard of a girl going all the way, to meet a boy who is a total stranger? What will people say? And, by the way, Binnie—in case you have forgotten, I was the one who had shortlisted the profile and while you both plan a cosy meet-up, I am being kicked out of the scene. Very good!*

For me, it was important to meet as and when convenient. I didn't have to rub my ego by insisting that he come to Delhi to see me.

Scene 5: Our first *date*

I wore a very simple but smart salwar-kameez and started for the chosen café, well in time. Little did I realise that the traffic in Bengaluru can be a spoiler for the mood and moment. Took me about two hours to reach the café! I made my way into the cafe exactly at 6 pm (an hour late) and looked around. Of course, I would have recognised Sri from his social profile pictures but I could not see him anywhere. At that moment, a message from Sri dropped in my phone inbox: *I will be 15 minutes late.* I sighed and waited.

Forty minutes later, I saw him coming out of a guest house across the road and walking leisurely towards the café. He was staying just 20 steps away from the cafe yet he was 40 minutes late! My mind was agitated. I kept mumbling to myself: *It's okay. I better ignore it!*

We sat down only to a dismal-looking Sri staring haplessly at me. I wasn't sure if he was dismayed on seeing me or was hungry for the last two days or was disappointed by the ambience of the café that he himself had chosen (on the recommendation of his *Bengalurean* friends).

What followed next was a detailed narration of agonies over his struggles while trying to re-settle in India. The saga unfolded, even as dismal pictures of the country were painted by him (accompanied by his dejected facial expressions)and tales told of the knee-deep mirth of corruption in the bureaucratic and banking circles and the frustrating delays he was encountering while handling the formalities of his four proposed start-ups.

I felt as if I was his private counsellor than a prospective alliance. The painful narration continued for the next one hour while the emotion of compassion scaled some high peaks in me and then, he abruptly stopped. The fact that we had not met for *therapy* probably struck Sri and he changed the gear, and steered in a direction as one ought to take while meeting up with a *could-be* partner-for-life. In the next hour or so, amiable talks were exchanged, future-goals were discussed, and orders of tea were repeated.

It all seems to be going somewhere or so, I thought.

It was time to leave. The moment froze as our eyes met briefly. After an awkward pause of two seconds, Sri broke the silence and suggested another meeting. *Let's meet again; let's explore the city together,* he said. I said that the next day was a busy one for me, owing to the full-day training that was scheduled. In a spirit of true valour, he offered to extend his visit to Bengaluru by another two days. Our eyes met again and with an unspoken emotion of admiration for each other, we bade *goodbye*.

The traffic seemed to be not much of a nuisance on my way back to the hotel. *Must be because I am re-living the moments of my rendezvous with Sri*, I thought. By the way, I also got a *did-you-reach* call, during which it was reinforced that *we should have spent more time together!*

Scene 6: The next day.

I remained busy in the training program and during the lunch hour when I checked my inbox,

I saw a message from Sri stating that he had to rush back to Hyderabad to complete his start-up(s) formalities—having arrived at an under-the-table understanding with the bank officials. I was nonplussed. *A meeting with bank officials on a Sunday? Oh, yes! Why not? It is convenient for nefarious deals to come knocking on weekends!*—I concluded.

Sri's promise to return the next day seemed sincere and stronger than the rocks I saw at Nandi Hills. *Wait for me, Leena... I will be back in less than 40 hours,* he had messaged.

Scene 7: 50 hours later.

Fifteen phone calls from me to him went unanswered. So, I sent messages to the effect: *What happened? Is everything okay? Did you get into trouble? Are you dead?*

I never heard back from Sri Ranganathan.

Scene 8: A full month later.

I arrive at a conclusion. *Probably, a coconut fell on the NRI's head when he returned to Hyderabad and he lost his memory....*

The last I hear of Sri is from his Facebook Status update: Scaling new heights at Orb zorbing, Essex & Suffolk Zorbing Park... Manningtree, United Kingdom and in a relationship with Monica Pandey!

Mr Americano Espresso

The second *laddoo* I encountered on my journey towards finding someone was…errr…*let me remember*…ah! No…oh, gosh! Ooops… *Was he Rohit or Mohit? How could I be so insensitive…don't even remember a guy's name?* Anyway… For reasons which shall gradually unfold—let us refer to him as *Mr Americano Espresso!* It is obvious he worked for the Americano Bank and about why the word Espresso comes to mind when I try to recollect his name? Well, that shall soon be known too.

Of course, I spent a few days sulking and ordering cheese margaritas and brownie shakes, after the first *laddoo* broke my heart. I did not even log on to the matrimonial site for a couple of weeks. However, the cheerful spirits bounced back when out of the blue, I got a call from a long-forgotten friend.

Nidhi: 'Hey Leena, wassup? Been so long, we need to catch up. But listen, today my call is really in connection with all the efforts I have been making to hook up a dear friend with a very sweet girl.'

On finding me unresponsive, she clarified: 'Stupid! Of course, the sweet girl is you!'

Me: 'Oh okay, I am listening.'

Nidhi: 'This friend—a spiritual health enthusiast and an orderly senior bank official with a disciplined routine—is in search of a soul mate. Just yesterday, he was at my place and it struck me, *Oh, my God! Leena & Espresso* will be an instant hit*! I told him about you and he seemed keen to connect with you. So, I thought why not check with you. Would you be interested in getting to know him?'

Even if a bit half-heartedly—I agreed to think over it. *Never say never without trying*!

Though it wasn't my cup of tea but I logged on to Facebook and did a bit of snooping and recce on the social networking channel about Mr Espresso.

Mr Espresso looked a little more mature than his age. *Is he really...really just 42? Umm... Some people go through a lot in life and all of it starts showing on the face.* I decided to be sympathetic. Not at his fittest best but thankfully, he had a tall frame, Mr Espresso looked decent. He had a wheatish complexion and seemed like the guy-next-door.

I called Nidhi a few days later and consented for my phone number to be passed on to Mr Espresso.

We were taught in school that light travelled faster than sound but guess, they had not met our Mr Espresso

---

* Of course, she had mentioned the actual name of the guy.

who was apparently faster than light! I said my *byes* to Nidhi and, in barely a minute—a WhatsApp message flashed on my screen.

Mr Espresso: 'Hey Leena, how are you? I am so happy to connect. Did you know "Leena" is an Irish word which means a wet meadow? I looked it up.'

The speed at which he had assumed a casual garb, hit me hard and I was knocked out.

Mr Espresso: 'Heeellloooooo... I can see you online. Why are you not typing? Hello! Leena?'

Me (after an effort to recover): 'I am fine. Yes, I am here.'

Mr Espresso: 'Hey, shall I call you now? You want to talk to me, isn't it? But, I am at work now. May I call you in the evening around 7 pm?'

Me: 'Okay.'

Sharp at 7 pm my WhatsApp notification buzzed...

Mr Espresso: 'Hey Leena, wassup?'

I remembered Nidhi's words: *Espresso is very particular and disciplined...* Of course, it showed!

After the usual barrage of *how are you, what do you do, what do you like to eat, what do you like to see*—I fell off the chair, when...

Mr Espresso: 'Do you know how to make *aloo-methi?* Can you guide me if I call you now? I picked up *methi* on my way, washed it, dried it...and chopped it but, now I need help to cook it.'

I felt as if I was connecting to my now-dead *Nani* who loved tormenting me by asking similar-sounding questions. I let that feeling pass.

Me: 'Hey Espresso, I am just average when it comes to cooking. Don't know much about complicated mixes and that includes *aloo-methi*.'

Mr Espresso: 'Oh, it is simple. Should I teach you?'

Wait, didn't you just say that you wanted me to guide you to cook this green-brown complex mix? The feeling of being taken-aback seemed to come in downpours, with him.

Mr Espresso (sensing my silence): 'Oh ho! I was merely testing you on your cooking skills.'

Excuse me! I wanted to shout back.

[Pause]

Mr Espresso: 'Okay... Okay. It is fine. So, tell me about your family.'

Me: 'Why?'

Mr Espresso: 'Tell me about your routine.'

Me: 'And, why would that interest you?'

Mr Espresso: 'What time do you wake up?'

Me: 'Sorry, I got to go! Catch you later.'

Espresso was not too happy on being cut out but, he put the chat to rest with a smiley.

Barely half-an-hour later, the WhatsApp notification buzzed once again.

Mr Espresso: 'By the way, the *aloo-methi* turned out super. Tomorrow, I will try *bhindi-aloo*.'

Me: 'Great! Happy cooking.'

My last thoughts before I slept: *Seems to be a nice guy. Yeah, a bit cheeky but, decent. Is it early to judge him? Should I talk a bit more?*

The thoughts were far too many, with the result that I forgot to keep my cell on the silent mode.

Beep! Beep! @ 4 am.

My snores were louder… I missed the beeps.

(It was a '*Good morning*' message when I checked it later.)

Beep! Beep! @ 4.45 am.

My snores were still louder.

Later, when I checked, Espresso's message was: 'Putting on my running shoes… I love the still mornings. Going for a walk.'

Beep! Beep! Beep! @ 5.30 am.

This time, the beeps were louder than my snores. I woke up with a start and a lot of fears came tumbling after: *Hope Ma, Pa, Bro, Chacha, Chachi, Maasi…all are fine.*

I pounced on my phone and nearly screamed: *STUPID!* $%***%$

The latest message was: 'What a lovely breeze outside! Have a great day!'

Beep! Beep! @ 7 am.

Mr Espresso: 'Are you still sleeping?'

I was sitting in my balcony...sipping masala chai, and enjoying the breeze. I did not reply.

Beep! Beep! @ 7.04 am.

Mr Espresso: 'Good morning! How are you, Leena?'

I was damn irritated by now. I replied calmly, though. The *yogi* inside me held my hands which would have otherwise smashed the phone with a force. I heard myself mumbling: *Shaaaaaantiiiiiii... Shanti!*

Me: 'Good morning! By the way, you wake up quite early!'

Mr Espresso: 'Yes, you see, I am particular about my walks. Moreover, I start for office at 7.30 am. Need to catch up on my health regime before that.'

Me (*wanted to write*): *But, I don't. I wake up at a time around which the normal half of the human race sets its morning alarm.*

However, I did not. Another rapid fire round of muttering *Ommmmmm Shaaaantiiiiiiii* ensued.

Me: 'Okay, good. Hey, I have to begin my day now. Let us connect later. Have a good day.'

Mr Espresso: 'Sure. Can I call you in an hour?'

Me: 'No, perhaps later.'

Mr Espresso: 'Okay.'

Two hours later...

Mr Espresso: 'Hey, wassup?'

One hour later...

Mr Espresso: 'Hey, wassup?'

Half-an-hour later...

Mr Espresso: 'Hey, can we talk?'

Me: 'Hey, I am busy. Can we talk later?'

One hour later...

Mr Espresso: 'Let me know when can I call.'

Twenty minutes later...

Mr Espresso: 'Going out for lunch. Let me know when can I call.'

Two hours later...

Mr Espresso: 'How is the day going for you?'

Me: 'Fine, you tell me... You seem to be pretty active on WhatsApp. Was it a light day for you?'

Mr Espresso: 'Oh, I know how to organise my day. I work by delegating. After all, it is also now important to take out time to know you.'

Me: 'Okay.'

Mr Espresso: 'Should we not meet once? How about tomorrow?'

I am taken aback for a while. I think furiously....

Me: *'Hmm...hmm...* Okay, tomorrow sounds fine.'

Mr Espresso: 'Lunch?'

Me: 'Okay.'

Mr Espresso: 'Let us meet at Crosspoint Mall. I want to take you to my favourite lunch place.'

Me: 'Okay.'

The next morning...

4.00 am: 'Good Morning.'

4.45 am: 'Going for my walk.'

5.30 am: 'Hey, can we talk?'

No prize for guessing who sent the above messages and to whom... I read them at 7 am.

Me @ 7.30 am: 'Hey, let us meet at lunch and talk.'

Mr Espresso @ 10 am: 'How is it going?'

Mr Espresso @ noon: 'Leaving office... See you in a while.'

At 12.30 pm, we meet in the parkway of the mall on Espresso's repeated insistence.

'You look so lovely! Thank you so much for coming. Oh, it is my lucky day!' Mr Espresso gushed.

Hmm... I have not got my eyebrows tweaked in a fortnight and my hair is in a mess, not to mention the dark circles my students have gifted me... Don't know what exactly he found lovely about me...I thought and said a polite, 'Thank you.'

'Hey, your bag is too heavy, I guess. Can I carry it for you?'

Espresso's hands almost tightened their grip on the straps of my handbag. I protested, 'NO (while almost snatching my bag), it is fine, I am used to carrying my weight around—on my own shoulders.'

Sniff!

Mr Espresso was visibly disappointed and muttered, 'As you say.'

Over the next two hours, Espresso's tales were drabber than the pasta we ordered. He just went on and on about how much he liked cooking; what he did at work and how meeting me that day had made it the brightest day of his life!

I could not take the monochromatic conversation any further and quickly offered, 'Hey, this has been nice. I got to go now. Got some evening plans.'

'Can't you stay for another hour?'

'No, I've got to go.'

'Okay... Can we meet for lunch tomorrow again?' Mr Espresso looked overtly eager.

Was I hallucinating? No... Leena, you can do it! Say it loud! Tell him what a buffoon you think he is... Ain't no mountain high enough! I managed a weak, 'I will let you know.'

'Dinner?' he shot back.

'I'll let you know.' I said a bit firmer this time.

'Lunch, day after?'

I kept silent.

'Oh, I think you are getting late. Let me drop you to your car.'

'No, thank you. I will be fine. Aren't you late for work?

'No, I was so excited to meet you that I took off for the rest of the day! I had more plans but you have to go,' he replied looking crestfallen.

My heart melted, and for an instant—I felt like pulling his cheeks and saying *'cho chweet'*, but the moment fortunately passed! I remained silent. I picked up my bag, and Espresso followed me saying, 'I will call you in the evening. Let us plan another meeting.'

'I have a meditation session to attend in the evening at an NGO. I will call you myself around 7 pm,' I countered quickly.

I got into the car and zoomed off to get a breather.

6.59 pm: Meditation centre

In the middle of an open-air meditation class, the sound of the flute was filling hearts and everyone was trying to connect with the breath. Suddenly, a phone rang!

I was rudely roused from the trance. I was aghast as it dawned upon me that the ringtone was familiar. The culprit was my cell phone. I dashed towards my bag in order to disconnect before the session went for a toss. Instead, the call got connected and to my utter embarrassment, went on speaker mode!

Mr Espresso chirped from the other end, 'Hey Leena, it is almost 7 pm. You did not call. I couldn't wait to talk to you.'

By then, everyone was abruptly thrown out of the elevated mode. They were all staring at me, confused.

I disconnected the call at that moment and switched it off. I told myself: *That's it! You interfered with my work despite a word of caution. You will pay for this, Espresso!*

I reached home with a temper hotter than the water boiling in the kettle and dialled Espresso's number. And then, what followed was a BLAST!

'What was the urgency to call when I had said that I would call at 7 pm?' I shouted over the phone.

'But you did not call until 6.59 pm. I was waiting,' Mr Espresso sounded taken aback.

'Enough of all this, Mister! You are such a clingy bag. My patience has been tested enough. Don't you have anything else to do? Have you even heard a phrase known to rational human beings called—*giving space*? What is the desperation and need to talk every hour? I like you but I cannot keep talking to you and interruptions at work TURN ME OFF. Had it not been for Nidhi, I would not have got myself into this.'

'But…errr…let me….'

'Not any more. I cannot handle this stalker kind of an attitude any longer. It was nice knowing you. Goodbye.'

'Did I come on too strongly to you? Good that you told me. I will slow down….'

There was dead silence on my end.

'Leena, let us talk tomorrow.'

'I just said… It was nice knowing you.'

'Buttttt….'

'That's it. I don't want to talk to you anymore. Please, do not call me. Thank you, and good luck!'

I disconnected the line.

My patience was, however, not yet fully tested. In less than five minutes, the message alert on my phone started beeping.

Mr Espresso: 'Hey, are you sure? Let us talk… I can change.'

I took the final and firm step.

Contact Status: Blocked!

The feeling of suffocation slowly receded, as the bubbles made a cheerful noise while I added *adrak* and *tulsi* in the chai.

I could now sip my tea in peace!

***Laddoo* II:** Case open and shut in 96 hours. *That was a quick exit!*

A Nostalgic Take Off

The next few weeks found me shrieking at the very sound of a message alert. Though I had blocked Mr Espresso's number, my fingers nevertheless trembled every time I flipped through the messages in the inbox, jittery of getting a spate of messages from him via some other number.

As luck would have it, an opportunity to immerse myself in work, found me. I was given the charge of organising a first-of-its-kind three-day Start-Up 1.0 Conference at the college, which involved intensive deliberations and collaborations between educational institutions and industry. I was the designated Convener and the next few days saw me spending time in the college till late in the evenings.

As I was finalising the list of speakers who were to be invited from the industry to address the students, a particular speaker's name and picture caught my attention. *Oh, this face looks familiar…and even this name. Where…where?* I mumbled to myself. I was sure that our paths had crossed some time. The name and profile stated: Chirag Vohra, Chief Technology Officer, Metromax, California, United States.

I was still lost in thoughts when the peon left a cup of tea on the table, and he did not get to ask how long I intended to keep him confined as well. And then, it hit me! *Of course, he is Chirag...* I burst out laughing, managing to save the cup from toppling over though a few drops of tea did spill over the dupatta.

Yes, the Chirag (even in the literary sense) of our school! The topper of the school, whom we unanimously disliked for he had given us all traumatic days and nights by virtue of his stupendous all-round performances. Though six years our senior, the parents of a large number of students in the successive batches had tried searching for or even planting similar sparks of brilliance in their own wards as were visible in Chirag. His was the picture and name shown to us (even as we were chided at being 'nowhere near him') from where it was framed and embedded on the Wall of Fame at school, and many a sleepless nights did we spend muttering not-so-decent verbal darts at him. And, on nights when we did manage to get a wink, we could prattle about his achievements if woken in the midst of our slumber—so much were his accomplishments drilled into our heads by the Principal during his annual speeches and otherwise. *Why did he have to do so well,* we had frowned thousands of times while passing through the corridors, as his picture looked down at us askance.

I picked up my bags and left for home a bit early that evening. The peon was grinning, and almost humming to himself. I was eager to share the crucial info with Mom. I entered the living room, and there she was glued to the soap opera being aired.

'Mom, guess what!' I began in full zest.

'Shhh... Wait for a while. Talk to me later. Bhanumati is going to turn into a cat any minute now,' she waved at me instructing me to stop, without as much as looking at me.

I decided I was not going to give in to some Bhanumati in a stupid soap!

'Mom, Chirag from the 1990 batch is coming to our college and will be one of the speakers at the conference,' I broadcasted in one go.

Of course, Mom turned around to look at me in lightning speed. 'Whaaaatttt! Chirag? What are you saying? After all these years! Oh, what a dear boy, he was!'

Mom started on a raving-about-Chirag spree, even as Bhanumati turned into a cat, amidst deafening sounds of bells and drums! Mom went on exclaiming about his brilliance and sighing over how ordinary my brother and I had turned out to be, in an alternate pattern.

I wasn't sure if the announcement was a good idea anymore.

From the next day onwards, I plunged myself in work and could not think of anything beyond the mammoth responsibilities ahead. The conference commenced, and concluded very well. I won generous accolades and notes of appreciation.

At the end of the valedictory session, as business cards were being exchanged over tea and refreshments, I walked up to Chirag and said, 'Hello, Mr Vohra! I am Leena, a faculty member. I must congratulate you for your brilliant presentation and equally inspiring Q&A session with the students. They loved it and have gained immensely from it.'

'Hello, Leena, nice to meet you as well. I have been watching you efficiently manage the affairs over the past three days. You have been flawless in every aspect. One of the best-organised conferences I have attended till date. And of course, it is a pleasure to interact with the young minds.' He sounded so very humble and earnest as he spoke, that I almost felt guilty for having called him unpleasant names while at school.

'Thank you, Mr Vohra.'

'Oh, you make me sound so old. Please, call me Chirag.'

'Okay, Chirag… By the way, I have to tell you this, we are from the same school.'

'Oh, is it? Remarkable, that is! Pardon me though, for I am unable to recollect. Were we in the same batch as well?'

'No, you were my senior. I was in the 1997 batch.'

'Aha, that is why... But I am so very pleased to connect with a schoolmate. Life certainly moves in circles,' laughed Chirag.

'Yes, I felt the same when I read about you and noticed your picture while listing down the speakers. It did not take me long to figure out that we were schoolmates...for you were quite well-known in school,' I added with a mischievous grin.

We went on speaking for an hour, at least. Thankfully, those in the reception committee were attending to the other participants of the conference and I could go on asking Chirag all that I wanted to know about him. I did feel intimidated by his towering persona in terms of his achievements. However, he made me feel at ease in no time. He was ordinary-looking; had average height and medium built; round, rimmed glasses and certainly not *handsome* by usual standards, but quintessentially intelligent and successful. I presumed he had a perfect life in a perfect place—California.

We reminisced about our former teachers and some of the stars of our school in sports and in the glamour quotient. We both found ourselves laughing and referring to our teachers with the same nicknames that used to go round the school. I did not realise when but I ended up giving him a few gossip bites as well and he too looked entertained with the juicy bits of information. I was astonished that *the* Chirag of our school was actually normal! *He too enjoys mischief and gossip,* I regaled myself.

I told him just a little bit about myself, for there was not much to tell. When I asked him about his work-profile, he sounded so very grounded and casual. The fact that he headed a high-powered team at Metromax, had least lessened his amiability. He casually shared that he was also very spiritually inclined and was involved with a lot of meaningful and philanthropic activities in the US as well as India.

It must have certainly been more than an hour. The delegates had begun leaving the auditorium and we realised that it was time to bid goodbye.

'I am happy that I could connect with you, Leena. I wish we had more time to chat. However, I need to go back and pack. Have an early morning flight tomorrow. I hope we can continue our conversation over e-mail or chat.'

'Sure, I would love to maintain the connection. I felt the same joy. Good luck and bon voyage, Chirag.'

'I wish you many good things in the days and months ahead too. Hopefully, you or some other institution organises a similar conference next year and invites me, and we get to meet again,' laughed Chirag and we shook hands pleasantly.

I was exuberant all the while as I wrapped up and assigned the concluding tasks to the teams of students. However, when I returned home, I was in a pensive mood. I was myself clueless when I tried thinking why. *What is bothering me? Why am I feeling this low? Did Chirag say something? I don't think so and the conference related work was also smoothly handled. Then, why?*

As I stared at the moonlit sky from the window that night I felt a rush of different emotions—each struggling to outdo the others. *Was I envious of the way life had turned out for Chirag?* We had not asked each other about our respective marital status but *he must be happily married with an intelligent wife and two brilliant kids,* I felt certain. Some lives move forth in a linear pattern and his seemed to be one such life. *Guess, this is what is troubling me,* I deduced.

It was not very often that I sat and brooded over my own life. But when I did that, the memories of the topsy-turvy ride that life had been, still generated fear in the gut. I could never forget how I had ushered in conscious changes in my being, over the past four years. I was a trendy and vivacious girl from Delhi, with an exciting life that hovered over my job, my boyfriend Lucky, shopping for clothes at CP, *chaat* at Kamala Nagar, happening parties, and time-pass at Palika Bazaar. Lucky was a stylish and overconfident boy from Delhi, with a carefree life. His life was all about oozing style while perched on a Bullet outside the South Campus of Delhi University, flaunting connections, planning the next rendezvous with girls and guys at *cool* restobars and animatedly discussing some *solid* business plans.

Lucky and I had married seven years ago, a little against the wishes of parents on both the sides. Consent apart, the marriage was nevertheless a *Delhi* wedding. Each side had incurred an expense of about Rs 50 lakhs, according to very conservative estimates. It had been a lavish five-day affair and since two of the celebrations were in a farmhouse near Mehrauli and two at Ashoka Hotel, it had managed to just about meet the laid-down standards of a *decent* Punjabi wedding. I, attired in a designer *lehenga,* had been bid adieu by my father in a brand new Toyota Corolla.

The romance and exuberance had lasted for about six months—approximately the same time that it took to exhaust the dinner invites extended by families and friends to us—the newlyweds. Lucky resumed negotiations and intense discussions on a couple of business plans with his friends who had both affluence and influence but lacked pragmatism and will. The plans never took off, and remained buried in the plush living rooms of the guys. Post-marriage, I continued with my job in college.

Two years passed and Lucky's miniscule efforts at executing his business plans remained too damp to succeed. He kept happily borrowing from his father and from me and surviving well. His lifestyle remained as flamboyant as ever... Another year passed, and signs of frustration were now visible in both our behaviours. I was exasperated while yielding to his consistent demands for money. My attempts at resisting the demands led to physical and emotional abuse. It had taken quite a while for me to come to terms with the reality of my marriage. By the time, I could legally step out of the wedlock—three years had passed and I too was no longer that same person as before.

During the months and years that followed, I and all those dear to me could see that I was falling into an abyss. That is when a sensible uncle practically forced me to register for a three-month yoga course. I was reluctant at first, for almost everything that was suggested to me by my well-wishers. Nothing appealed to me, and I just did not want to do anything. I wanted to simply retreat in a shell and lie dormant for a while. Doing a full-time yoga course, seemed to be taking me towards that cocoon wherein I could hide safely for some time. I registered myself for the course and as the sessions progressed, I took to the yoga lessons so very completely and naturally that I myself was amazed at my new-found thoughts and conduct.

Looking intently at the moon, I retraced my steps and brought myself to the present. I knew that while a few depressing thoughts were causing a temporary clutter in the mind, the thoughts would ease in a while.

I decided to join Mom in the living room and find out what happened after Bhanumati turned into a cat! I wanted to know if her husband had recognised her.

A Rap

Mom decided to go a little gentle on me for the next few days. I basked in the comfort of her care and indulgence. That day, however, she was unusually gentle. Her heart seemed to have gone on an extra-soft mode, as she lovingly placed a giant-sized, round and fluffy *bhatura* on my plate at lunch time.

'Binnie, don't work too hard, *beta*. You should take things easy. Go out with your friends, take morning walks, or go for movies in the evenings and unwind yourself... Do you want to do a short getaway with me?'

This is leading somewhere... I instantly pressed the alert button and my antennas popped out, to spot and thwart any danger lurking out there.

'Thanks, Mom. I know I need to go out sometimes but not now. I am busy with the district eliminations of the Annual Debate Festival to be held in our college.'

'Okay, that is fine dear. But, whenever you can, you must go and enjoy yourself.'

'Hmm....'

'Binnie, do you remember Mrs Shah, our former neighbour who moved to Kenya five years ago?'

Ah! Now, she is talking.

'Yes, Mom. I do.'

'Well, she called this morning. Believe me, such a sweet lady she is... She casually happened to mention a friend of her son, who moved back to India last year.'

'Okay?'

'According to Mrs Shah, he is a one-in-a-million kind of a guy. He has had a divorce. He was educated in Kenya and lived there for about eight years before shifting to Delhi to take care of their family business. He lives with his parents, while his elder sister is married.'

'Mom, please. Let me enjoy my lunch.'

Placing the next *bhatura* on my plate, Mom continued, 'He is well read, and besides, he is settled in Sainik Farms. Binnie, Sainik Farms! Just think about it. Isn't it perfect? Is it not every Delhi girl's one secret wish that she be handed over in matrimony to some prince from South Delhi? His age is perfect; has no children; is fair and not even bald; and is neither very tall, and nor very short... The only thing is that he has a bulging middle. But, Mrs Shah said he is a polite and chivalrous guy. Do we need to know more?'

'Mom, do you seriously think that we ought to be arriving at conclusions or opinions on the basis of what Shah Aunty says?'

'Mrs Shah is so kind...she is even worried for you. Here, take this *malai-sandwich* I have tried today after ages... Well, she gave me Shakti's number. I saw his profile picture on WhatsApp. I can tell you he certainly exceeds our expectations. I told Mrs Shah that you will connect with Shakti tonight.'

'Shakti? What a name, Mom!'

Before I could air my opinions further on the guy in the fray (from our end), Mom dashed out of the room and left me pining for more...*malai-sandwich*!

Mom forwarded me the number, as I discovered after dinner. There was that familiar stern little instruction that always accompanied any telephone number she forwarded of these sorts. I checked him out on WhatsApp. *Not an impressive profile picture. Mom always exaggerates! He may be good looking but is stone-faced... And, what's with so many rings on his fingers? Don't think there is room for an engagement ring to fit anywhere!*

Well, time to proceed further....

@9 pm

Me: 'Hey Shakti. This is Leena. Shah Aunty had suggested that we connect.'

Next day @9 am

Shakti: 'Hi Leena, am sorry. I could not reply earlier. When you messaged last night, I was busy in prayers.'

Me: 'That is fine. How are you?'

Shakti: 'I was not fine this morning but ever since I read my forecast for the day which said that *I will feel very energetic today*, I feel absolutely alright. Also, it said that the next one hour is an auspicious time to chat with a strange girl. I hope you can spare some time to talk?'

[Pause]

Me: 'Yes, okay, fine.'

Shakti: 'Let me call you then.'

Soon, he called me on WhatsApp and I picked up the call with much anticipation, 'Hello, again. Do you believe in forecasts?'

An ungiving babyish voice which felt as if it would anytime switch over to a sermon-giving mode came from the other end. 'Yes, I very much believe that everything in our lives is pre-destined. Yet, situations often get disturbed due to the wrong positions of and conflict between our stars. If we take the right measures at the right time, life moves smoothly. *Shivoham! Shivoham!* Hang on...give me a moment to finish my glass of juice.'

Dook… dook… dook…sluuuurrrrrppppp!

I wanted to ask, *Has the time to drink the juice been forecasted in the paper too?* Instead, I kept quiet.

'Are you God-fearing, Leena?' Shakti asked me.

Now, what is this all about? I exhaled deeply. 'I am spiritually inclined and strong in my faith. However, I do not follow rituals or believe in established ceremonies.'

Shakti's voice became feebler as he said, 'Sad to know that. I am a Shiva *bhakt*. I zealously pray twice a day—morning and evening. Every weekend, I go to a Shiva temple. My family is also one of the trustees of the temple board. We frequently donate towards the upscale of the temple building. Whosoever marries me should be open to adopting the family culture as soon as she can. The sooner she adopts, better it shall be for all of us. *Shivoham! Shivoham!*'

I wondered if I was speaking with a weird-sounding Baba. *Should he rather not remain unmarried, immersed as he is, in the service of God?* 'Okay. Nice. I am of the view that we are all free to follow and do what we like.'

'After we are done talking, please send me your horoscope. I have an excellent software for match-making. It will tell us exactly how many of our respective stars match,' offered Shakti.

I knew I was going to ignore his request. If he bypassed me and directly approached the High-Command *(Mom, of course)*, I could predict what would happen next!

He did not wait for me to affirm or deny his request. He continued, 'Leena, I was living a carefree life in Kenya. I had everything at my disposal; everything that a young man yearns for—girls, parties, a fat pay package, junk food, cars, expensive watches… I could buy all that I desired but…but my life was not taking me anywhere. There were those moments when I felt completely useless and frustrated. During such times, I wondered as to why was I not happy. Then one day, Lord Shiva came in my dream. He asked me to leave the foreign land and let go of the *moh* and *maya*…the superficial diversions of the fickle mind and come back to India and spend my life in the service of the Lord and of my parents. The dream was so powerful that it gave me a new-found faith in the divine power of Lord Shiva. I moved to India last year, took over the reins of our family business and now, I feel fine. Our company's profits have doubled in this one year with His blessings. *Shivoham! Shivoham!*'

'Hmm… But tell me, is there nothing that frustrates you anymore?' I asked him.

After a long pause, Shakti replied, 'No, I still do feel frustrated sometimes when my stars are not in perfect alignment. You see, when I fall sick, or when a deal does not get through or when I end up having a fight with Dad, I feel frustrated. But then, I also immediately become aware that I must have unintentionally done something to upset my Lord Shiva or my stars are in conflict that day.'

I was feeling dizzy now and almost spotted a star or two before my eyes in the day. I asked, 'Then, what do you do?'

'Then I sit to pray. I pray, pray and pray. Things become fine again. That is…that is the power of my Lord Shiva. *Shivoham! Shivoham!*'

He continued, while I found myself mumbling *Shivoham…Shivoham*, too!

'I want to start a family soon after marriage.'

Hey, hold on! What a jump from one topic to another… It has barely been five minutes of chatting… Are you riding a flying horse? Instead, I said, 'At this moment, I would not like to get married just to have kids.'

'Well, this poses a problem because I am a very family-oriented person.'

'That is good. To me, "family" also includes the beautiful companionship between two people, before the kids come into the picture. To have a family cannot just mean producing kids; it also means to first build on and have a close bond with the partner.'

In a dismissive tone, Shakti said, 'You see, I got a premonition while I was meditating one day, that my child will be gifted; a special boon from Lord Shiva. In fact, I am already getting a room refurbished as a baby room in my house. My sister is designing it.'

'That is nice,' I replied. 'But you must realise that each one must make his or her choices and decisions.'

'It is this feminism and all the related nonsense about *living-your-life mantra* that is ruining our society. Women are taking absurd decisions. Either they don't want kids or they want to adopt. I think a woman is not complete until she becomes a mother. Look at our mothers, our grandmothers... They embraced motherhood so naturally. More the advancements, more is the nuisance. We were better off before this digital age. At least, our women talked some sense,' he offered.

I couldn't stop myself. I said, 'I insist that you do not take upon your humble self to list down all that women must do or not do and also refrain from the trouble of casting your judgement on what they did or did not do in earlier times.'

He was unrelenting and said, 'But, it is a fact. You are afraid of the truth, I guess. It disturbs me that more and more women do not want to have children. This is just not right. You must first tell me categorically, whether you will have kids or not?'

'So, this is how you think? All the best with your road-map for child production, Shakti... I suggest that you take a swift route to your destination, or you may miss the bus, considering your age as well. And I pity the girl who would be your partner in the production process, for she may not have much else beautiful in wedlock to look forward too.'

There, I had said it. Of course, he began with a, 'Hoowwwwww can you?'

But I stopped him in the middle, 'I would like to conclude this chat now. I do not think that we are on the same page here. Thank you for calling, Shakti.'

'I will pray for you, Leena. You should change your mentality. May you not waste this life by remaining an incomplete woman... *Shivoham... Shivoham!*' He managed to get in before the call was disconnected.

My eyes were stinging with all those piercing remarks of his. I pensively mused for the next several minutes on the kind of convictions people so very self-assuredly but insensitively harboured.

I was not the chosen one to give birth to the gifted Shaktiman Jr! Most likely, a fault in my stars—I chuckled to myself.

I wondered if John Green had had a similar encounter when he wrote: 'There is no shortage of faults to be found amid our stars.'

Mom and I quickly forgot Shakti.

Mrs Shah became too busy to call upon Mom as frequently as she did earlier.

Chants of *Shivoham, Shivoham*… followed by uncontrollable bouts of laughter rocked our living room for many days.

The Saga of the 3 am Guy

Days flew by and the dosage of Mom's one-liners-aimed-at-emotional-blackmail was sustained at two-three times a day, or as directed by Pummy Aunty.

One lazy Sunday afternoon, the above dosage finally yielded results and I reluctantly agreed to once again sift through the profiles shortlisted by Mom, following her laborious rummaging on *shaadi-ka-laddoo.com*

Here was this one, given a four-star rating by Mom: 38-year-old handsome Punjabi boy, born in Delhi, settled in London, loves to read and seeks a simple, homely Punjabi girl.

Am I homely? I wondered for several minutes but didn't find an answer.

Suneet had a strange *I-am-sorry-to-be-born* look. He had a light, creamy complexion, broad forehead, and a rotund abdomen. He had posted about eight profile pictures on his account: one full size; one seated on a bike; one with an M&S shopping bag; another with his shades... I was irritated and yet I kept scrolling and there was this last one in his high-end gym gear.

'Mom, I don't have a very good feeling about this guy, Suneet,' I tried to warn Mom.

Mom, with raised eyebrows, exclaimed, 'Why, what is wrong with Suneet? I don't see any glaring default in his physical appearance or in his profile. He goes to the gym but I think he must have taken some package deal. Trainers don't focus much on those who take some cheap package. Perhaps, you can help him work on his belly and recommend some *yogasanas*.'

She winked at me as she said the last line. *Unbelievable!*

'Mom, he has a weird, hangdog look on his face,' I protested.

'Leena, don't be too disapproving all the time and that too without even meeting the guy in person. Yogi Satya Shri Guru says: "Let your fingers always point at yourself." Now, come on...get going!'

I accepted the request to connect.

Two hours later, I received a reply and it was the beginning of another *laddoo's* saga.

Suneet: 'Hey Leena, thank you for accepting my request to connect. How are you?'

Me: 'I am fine. How about you?'

Suneet: 'I am good... Do you want to take this chat on the cell? It will be a bit more convenient.'

Me: 'Hmm…why not.'

The instant we exchanged our numbers, there was a WhatsApp flash.

Suneet: 'Hey, I am Suneet. So much nicer here.'

Me: 'Hey Suneet, Leena here. Yes, I know.'

Suneet: 'Leena, guess both of us are in search of a soul mate and this has brought us to *shaadi-ka-laddoo.com*… So, tell me about yourself.'

The next few messages we exchanged were a repetition of the drill: *what do I do, where was I born, what do I like*…and *blah, blah, blah* from the other end too.

Suneet: 'Can I call you? I feel talking is the best.'

My tired fingers couldn't agree more with his idea!

Two minutes later, we were talking on the phone.

'Hey Leena, thank you for talking with me.'

Thank you? Why is he thanking me? Hey, are you okay?—I wanted to ask, instead I accepted the gratitude, 'Of course.'

'So, you live in Gurgaon? My family is also settled there.'

'Okay, so, do you visit India often?'

'Yes, once every year. In fact, the last year I came down twice.'

A pause followed. He had emphasised the word *twice* and thereafter seemed to have vanished in thoughts faraway.... 'Hey Suneet, all well? You seem to be lost somewhere.'

'It may sound awkward but in this past one year, I visited two times only to be fooled by a girl. Hey, do not mind but want to ask you if you are sure you want to settle down and not just pass some time—chatting with guys?' He was almost whispering now.

Oh, no! A bruised case! I rubbed my forehead vigorously and uttered a deep, long sigh! 'Of course, I know what I want.'

'You know, these Delhi girls are just too much! Of course, I do not mean you when I refer to the girls from Delhi. They are not sure of what they want in life or I guess, they are sometimes too sure of what they want but we fools—the guys, can never understand what they really want. Can I share something with you?'

I almost opened my mouth to voice my protest on what he had to say for the petite and innocent girls from Delhi, but then decided otherwise on second thoughts. *Why do I need to educate a man I don't know, on the virtues and credibility of us girls from Delhi? Moreover, technically, wasn't Gurgaon outside the boundaries of Delhi? Hence, no need to react,* I told myself.

Meanwhile, his voice was barely audible as he shared the experience which had obviously left a scar. I strained my ears far too much, and mumbled to myself: *Am I in for another episode of being an Agony Aunt?*

I tried to wriggle myself out. 'But, why do you want to share with me a personal experience? We have barely spoken for ten minutes.'

After a really long sigh, he continued, 'There is something in your voice…a calming effect…a reassurance that I sense… I feel I should tell you… Haven't felt this instant connect with anyone in a long time; you sound very kind.'

Bingo! There is another awkward pause.

'Okay, Suneet, if you feel so… Go on!'

The saga began… I thanked God for a small mercy—that it was a Sunday!

'I met this girl online, on the same matrimonial site which has brought us together. She was very sweet and charming…everything looked perfect; everything seemed to fall in place. We started chatting for hours every day…sent good morning hugs and good night kisses… There were those: *did you eat* and *why did you not eat* routine drills… I started calling her *Baby doll*…and she called me *Shona boy*… This went on for two months. One day, when I asked her if we should meet—she replied, "Oh, my Shona boy…that is a wonderful idea but you are in London,

I stay in Delhi." I told her, "No worries, Baby doll… I will fly down to Delhi…let us spend some time together."

Every time, he said *Baby doll* or *Shona*, I felt an eerie sensation in my being… I felt creepy, being involuntarily dragged into what seemed to be a freakish tête-à-tête. There was not an iota of sympathy generated in me… I was trying, nevertheless. In such situations, my PG Wodehouse can be trusted for putting the exact sentiment in just the right words. I searched a few quotes on Google while simultaneously listening to the creepy story of Suneet and pat popped up a hilarious one:

'There is a certain stage in the progress of a man's love when he feels like curling up in a ball and making little bleating noises if the object of his affections so much as looks squiggle-eyed at him.' I wanted to excuse myself for a minute and laugh out loud but the sense of pity in me did not let me.

Suneet continued, 'I packed my bags in full gusto to meet my *Baby doll*… And Leena, I must tell you that though I am settled in London, I did not forget my Punjabi roots and bought an expensive watch for my *Baby*. At the airport, we were elated to see each other… Errr, now when I look back, I think she was more delighted to see the watch! Anyhow, that moment I felt quite proud of myself, for she was so happy to see the gift. I told her at the airport, "Let us meet tomorrow. We will sit down over coffee and chat…" My *Baby doll* replied, "Oh no, Shona…let us watch a movie and go for shopping."'

Talking of watches, I looked at the watch on the wall. It seemed to be deliberately inching slowly that day. Mom had quietly peeped in a few times in that hour, smiled and while leaving, kept the door ajar. She did not know that I had seen her comings and goings in the mirror in front of me. I decided that the next time she popped up to check on me—I was going to ask her to get a cup of coffee with some yummy snack so as to not doze off, while the saga continued… *While I talked to her prospective son-in-law, she was going to get me anything I asked for,* I knew it. I began to ruminate whether asking Mom for samosas along with mango milkshake would be a good idea!

I had not missed a word, meanwhile.

Suneet countinued to pour out his woes, 'The next day, we watched a movie and though I was tired, she made me take tedious rounds of GK 1 and South-Ex markets… My International credit card, being unused to such an overload of purchases—was also exhausted! She bought perfumes, clothes, shoes, make-up…and what not! I just remember the message I received that day on my cell phone: *Thank you for using your credit card for 300 Pounds today.*

Over the next three days, the smart babe from Delhi kept celebrating my visit by shopping, dining out at expensive restaurants and giving me hugs of hopes. My idea to sit down and talk with her about our future plans was deflated quietly.

Errr…are you listening, Leena? Am sorry, I did not mean to generalise when I referred to girls from Delhi as smart babes.'

There was silence for the next few seconds.

'Hellllooooooooo…are you there?' He asked a little hesitantly.

I was part-tired, but still amused and curious to know the saga in its entirety. I also wanted him to feel guilty about referring to the girls from Delhi—the way he did. I just said, 'Hmm…'

He took that as the green signal to go on, and the trace of hesitation in his voice vanished instantaneously as he continued. 'On the fourth day, I called her up and decided to speak with her. Because whenever we met, her coy glances…sweet smiles…and the fluttering of her eyelids left me speechless—not to mention the bills which the shops and restaurants kept handing me down. As soon as she took my call, she started off, "Oh, my Shona, do you think we can go to the bridal exhibition at the Ashoka Hotel today? I believe some exclusive pieces are displayed there."

I mustered my courage and decided to take the matter head-on. I told her, "Baby, don't you think, we need to first talk about our future? Let us meet each other's families. I also have to go back and resume work." She, however, was just not ready for it. She said I was a nice guy but she did not think it was the right time to meet the parents yet. And then...then....'

I heard him sniffing. *Was he sobbing? Poor guy... The soul-testing experience had left the poor bloke overwrought.* Precisely then, Mom entered the room with samosas and *elaichi* chai and a smile to top it all... Her hopes were soaring, considering the number of hours I was talking with this Punjabi NRI guy! *I could have asked for anything today,* I reminded myself. She left me to savour the samosas and the saga and I was confused about prioritising them. I first took a bite into the *matar-jeera-aloo* samosa and then turned to the poor guy's ordeal. 'Are you alright? I say, let it be. You do not have to recollect the vexing episode. Let it go... We can talk about something else.'

'No...no...no... I want to tell you all. I am finding it soothing—sharing my pain with you... When I insisted with her that we should take the matter further, her exact words were: "You see, I like you but I do not feel that there is any spark amidst us yet. Why don't we talk a little more and take this slowly? Also, I think you need to do something about your weight. I find you fat! Anyway, I got to go now. The exhibition at Ashoka is not something which happens every day," and saying so she left me with a badly bruised and broken heart.'

The poorly crushed *Shona* had apparently spent the next two days sulking before flying back to London and resuming his mechanical routine—and this he revealed while muttering intermittently between sobs. What an end to a blossoming love story! *But hey! Are we at 'the end'*? I assumed so but—apparently, it was not all.

'Oh that is sad! What a terrible end!' The light-hearted nonchalance in my tone would not have escaped his sombre counterpart.

But Suneet promptly interrupted, 'No...no...it did not end there.'

'What? Is there more to it?' I was dreading the answer.

'Yes, after reaching London—I sent umpteen messages to my *Baby doll,* but they all went unanswered. After three months, I returned to Delhi. In those three months, I embarked on a crash diet and spent my evenings doing intense workouts in a gym in London. I messaged the flight timings and a selfie in my shrunk size and requested her to see me at the airport.'

'Well, was she there?' The samosas and chai had energised me...but so had the *smart ways* of the smart Delhi girl.

'Yes, she was there at the airport. She hugged me lovingly and exclaimed, "Hey, wow…somebody is looking hot! When I saw your selfie, I could not believe that it was my own Shona boy!" But I could sense that her eyes were searching for something else. And I, being in a state of delusion, handed her a necklace I had bought for her. Her eyes lit up, and a tighter hug enveloped me. Her swooning expressions left me happily nestled in that state of delusion. This time she initiated the talk about meeting her family and I happily agreed. I was jubilant that all of it was leading somewhere! We spent a day happily shopping and going to places and having a good time… The next day, I was supposed to meet her family. At about 11.30 that night, she messaged mesaying, "I don't think it is going anywhere… I am not sure what I want. Let us call it off. Bye." Leena, am sure that a kind person such as you can imagine how shattered I must have been….'

There were loud sobs from the other end. Even the most hard-hearted would have experienced surging waves of sympathy, on hearing an innocent *Shona*'s suffering at the hands of a smart *Baby doll!* After this second heartbreak, poor *Shona boy* returned to London with a broken heart and a mounting credit card bill.

'I am sorry to know about this experience of yours, Suneet.' *Fathead!* I said in a hushed whisper.

'Can I ask you something, Leena?'

There was a pause. Obviously from my end… 'Yes, you may.'

'Why do girls behave like that?'

'Well, I don't really know but, come on, Suneet… Cheer up! It is time to begin afresh!'

'Yes, you are right. It has been lovely talking with you. Must compliment you on your patience and sweet voice.'

'It's quite late now. Let us chat another time.'

Another time came up in less than 24 hours.

There were generous showers of compliments: *your voice is so sweet; you sound so balanced; my mother would love to meet you…whoever marries you will be a very lucky man,* and the like.

I had barely begun sympathising and even liking the compliments a bit when they already started sounding too artificial and stuffy.

Two days later:

Suneet: 'Hey, do you know in no time you have left such a wonderful impression on my mind that I woke up at 3 am today thinking about you and then looked you up on the internet… What say, shall I come to Delhi next month?'

I woke up at 3 am today thinking about you—his words kept ringing in my ears, and gave me a weird feeling. *Why the hell did he think of me at 3 am and looked me up on the internet?* All kinds of thoughts began racing and galloping in my mind.

From there on, it kept getting weirder… The messages kept coming at all hours and the sweet nothings he wrote seemed freakish to the core. And the monologues from his end never made any attempt to draw me into the conversations. I realised I had hardly ever *spoken* with him. I had just been a mute listener at the other end. One evening, when Suneet called, and before he could shower another compliment or book his ticket to Delhi, I politely told him that I was closing the chapter.

As expected, an emotional outburst (directed at '*you Delhi girls*') of a terrible kind followed, through which I patiently held myself. I wanted to apprise him with the technical and geographical fact which clearly established that I was not from Delhi but, he did not give me an opportunity.

'How can you do this to me? No, you cannot; you just cannot. I was so very much hoping to come and see you. I have also bought a gift for you. Am not complaining about the money I spent on the gift but you cannot do this… You know whoever will marry you, will be a very lucky man….'

I disconnected before the sobs turned louder... The gloomy googlies of this *laddoo* had bowled me over.

An Indrawn Escapade

I was super excited about visiting London and the Lake District. I had finally made up my mind to tick off the first two listings on my bucket list.

For me, one of those long-lasting childhood memories that find a cosy place to nestle forever in the heart was of my enchantment with the books penned by Beatrix Potter. The magical world she weaved for children was my safe haven in all times of trouble throughout my teenage. As youth bade goodbye to the teens, *The Daffodils, The Solitary Reaper* and the other works of Wordsworth enthralled me. Naturally, visiting the Lake District (about five hours from London) was numero uno on my bucket list—for both my superstars belonged there. I wanted to breathe the air which had filled their words with colour and spirit and tread on the soil graced by their footprints. Even London had a special place in my heart. Its tryst with history intrigued me; and the sights of its charm and beauty (till then seen on TV) held me captive. I also had this recurring dream which found me doing yoga on the plush greens of the Kensington Gardens.

'I am going to London and the Lake District this summer break,' I declared at the dinner table even as I anticipated a flustered reaction from Mom to the breaking news! But, she bowled me over when she exclaimed a cheerful 'Aha!'

I was not sure if this was her real and final reaction or was she biding time to equip herself with the canons.

'What! You are okay with it? Let me tell you that I propose to take this trip all by myself and not join any "Ladies only" group tour and dare you not ask any of our cousins to join me. And let me also inform that I intend to relax for two full weeks.' I looked at the three faces—Mom's, Papa's and Shaurya's—sitting around, in anticipation. Of course, the very next minute, I received three distinct reactions—so much so that I need not even specify who said what.

Reaction 1: 'Wonderful! What a terrific vacation you will have! You are finally thinking about your own dreams and wishes... By the way, what will you get for me?'

Reaction 2: 'Okay, what can we say if you have already made up your mind? It would have been nice though if you had asked me as well, to join you.'

Reaction 3: 'I'm happy, *beta*... You need a break and you also get to fulfil a big desire of yours. If you need anything, do let me know. I will arrange for a supplementary credit card for you, just in case....'

With a coy smile on my face and butterflies in my stomach, I started shopping and packing excitedly. Stepping inside the *Dove Cottage* of Wordsworth had always been one of those distant dreams that one does not expect to become a reality. After all, my means were subsistent and life, simplistic. My dreams did not torment me; rather they amused me. I remained happy even after I had done dreaming and did not sigh wistfully while stepping into the real world. Whether it was wise or not to never struggle against the odds, for turning my dreams into a reality, I don't know. My dreams never pushed me; never gave me sleepless nights. In fact, I slept fitfully after daydreaming about my would-be escapades....

Life was going good. I was content and deeply enjoying my yoga sessions in the evenings with a cross-section of students. There were the senior citizens and then there were expectant mothers and of course, what a delight it was to teach the tiny toddlers! I was in regular touch with Chirag, who had almost become a *good* friend, over the months. We exchanged e-mails though they still largely pertained to social, educational, industrial or even national and international affairs. Sometimes, we exchanged a new idea if either of us had one or we just exchanged pleasantries, and sometimes, I sought his counsel when students needed an expert advice or a wise input. We never discussed personal matters but then there were times when even I allowed my curiosity to wander unleashed.

Mom's persistent efforts at getting me re-settled by way of matrimony, often left me nervous though. Now that I had caved in and registered myself at *shaadi-ka-laddoo.com,* there was a spring in her steps. Despite the earlier episodes going awry, her spirits remained high. On some days, I grumbled quietly and on other days, I flared up a little but did dutifully go through the proposals Mom asked me to. However, this one time, I had kept from her the fact that I had been talking to a guy I had found interesting while flipping through the profiles listed on the site. Incidentally, he lived in London. *Was this desire to finally take this trip to London coincidental?*

A month after the *Shona-Baby Doll* incident, Saurabh's interesting profile had caught my attention. My first reaction was: *Wow, he is handsome!* Though I had never affixed any image in my mind as far as looks were concerned, but I must admit that I felt an instant attraction as I looked at Saurabh's profile picture. *Is it because he is almost six years older to me? Does his photo ooze a feeling of self-assuredness and is this what I am seeking in men? Or, is it the boyish grin and the dimpled cheeks that have bowled me over?* He had a well-conditioned body, stood tall at 5 feet 9 inches and had a perfectly chiselled face.

He lived alone in London, while his parents and sister were settled in Canada. He was a management consultant and quite highly placed in an MNC. He was also a yoga practitioner and a believer in the karmic philosophy. I was initially a little guarded in my responses. I did not want to plunge into something with very high expectations and then regret it later.

Saurabh sounded very humble, sensitive and mature in the conversations that we had begun having. I gradually found myself speaking with him effortlessly for hours. We laughed freely and spoke on almost everything that touched our lives during the day. He was a very well-read person and his thoughts seemed to be fairly evolved too. I did not ask him the reason for his single status, though I had given to him the details of my failed marriage.

About two months ago, we expressed a mutual desire to finally meet up.

In good humour, Saurabh had one day said instantaneously, 'Hey, why don't you come over to London? You seem to have a passion to visit the city, even otherwise, isn't it?'

I was taken aback, but joining him, I too had replied in a lighter vein, 'Wow! That would be wonderful, isn't it? Are you sure you want me to come? Because, I just might....'

'Of course, yes... I am sure. Why don't you enquire about the tickets and visa from a good travel agent? Let us meet and take the relationship forward,' Saurabh had sounded more confident than ever.

For the next two days, I had mulled over the prospect of going to London and the Lake District—examining every pro and con of it. Of course, I could not explicitly tell Mom and Papa that one reason for taking the trip was to meet a guy I had met online. Fortunately, there was also the fact that the two places were at the top of my bucket list... Determined, I decided to take the risk and explore what life had in store for me.

I felt a bit dizzy at times, with all of it happening so fast. I was excited and yet, there were the spates of fear gripping me. *Am I doing the right thing? Should I be going this far to meet a stranger?* I wondered often.

Just to keep someone trustworthy in the loop, I decided to write to Chirag about my travel plans. I knew he would not ask me the *whys* and *hows;* he would not, in fact, ask anything. I wrote him an e-mail, informing him that I was going to be in the UK on the said dates. I asked him politely if he was going to be in Europe at that time and if it would be possible to meet. Chirag wrote back a cheerful reply, egging me on to live my dream. He, however, regretted that he was going to be away in Shanghai during the period. The fact that I had not told him the real reason behind the trip left me uncomfortable for several hours. I decided to be honest with him. However, I had never apprised him until then with personal details. This resulted in many deleted messages on WhatsApp.

The dilemma was snowballing inside me when Chirag called up the next morning. It was drizzling pleasantly, and I was lazing on the arm-chair with a cup of tea. Mom and Papa had left early in the morning for a *kirtan* in my maternal uncle's house. Shaurya had left for college.

'Leena, may I ask if something is the matter? Do you want to talk?'

'No, it's just that… I… I do not know what to say and where to begin.'

'What happened? Are you alright? You seemed pretty delighted yesterday at the prospect of fulfilling one of your dreams.'

'Yes, I am very happy now that I have precious moments to look forward to and memories to make. It's just that there is a whole lot to it than what I have told you.'

'Do you wish to share?'

And I narrated the entire story of my personal life to him. He listened with great understanding and gave a few empathetic comments at the right moments. I felt light and relieved as never before. He did not judge me, and rather cautioned me against taking anything far too seriously in life. He favoured an amused outlook towards people and life; a spectator's perspective was often an ideal one, he said. We both managed to laugh heartily by the time I had finished telling him of my encounters on *shaadi-ka-laddoo.com.*

To find a true and unbiased friend at any point of time in life, who accepts us unconditionally, is akin to unexpected pennies from heaven! I looked up and thanked God for the windfall.

After breaking the news at home and a fortnight before my departure, when I called Saurabh to give him the happy news that I had booked my tickets, there was an awkward silence at the other end.

I was too excited then (or stupid?) to take note that he had taken a couple of minutes before responding guardedly, 'Oh, is it so? When are you coming? How come you decided all of a sudden? You never mentioned! We could have discussed it together.'

I had registered none of the reluctance or the slight irritation in his voice as he spoke. I had interpreted the barrage of questions as indicative of he being taken by surprise.

I texted him the flight details and resumed my preparations. I spent a lot of time thinking about the gift I wanted to carry for him. After having decided on and then discarded a couple of options, I finally settled on two books—one on poetry and the other on philosophy.

Two days prior to my departure, it did strike me odd that Saurabh had not called or replied to my messages for more than a week. I had not initially paid heed to this strange behaviour on his part. Since the past two months, we had been chatting every single day. When the lack of communication from his end did strike me, my heart missed a beat for an instant. *What if…*a sudden rush of fearful thoughts emerged from nowhere and clamoured to enter my mind. The next instant, I firmly shook my head and brushed them all aside. *No, it cannot be… No, there is nothing to worry… I know him so well. He must be busy at work*—I convinced myself and decided to focus on my to-do list.

Saurabh had called just once before I boarded the flight. I was more careful and did note that he was not his usual self. I was confused. A rush of thoughts were flooding my head: *Was he cold or was he just tired due to the pressures at work? Why was he not excited? Well, no…maybe he is not able to express himself clearly. Of course, he must be waiting too. For how long could we have just chatted online? He has developed cold feet, probably. Guys do get nervous, isn't it? It will all be well, once we meet.*

I boarded the flight and reached Heathrow at about 9 pm local time. I had seen him live on video chat every day for two months and hence, I was sure I would not have to make an effort to spot him. My eyes searched for that one familiar face, at first eagerly, then anxiously and finally, with a sinking heart—the eyes finished their scanning. *No, he is not here,* they told my weary heart. I had been praying during the journey that may I not be in for any shock. *And yet, here is the first one*—I shook my head and walked out of the terminal.

I am so glad that I have an itinerary all worked out, and that no major plan of mine shall go awry. I will give the gifts to someone worthy. I have a hotel to go to, and well, I will make the most of the rest of my tour too, I tried to put up a brave front.

I had been so sure that Saurabh would excitedly take me first to his apartment and that despite my jet lag, we would talk endlessly for hours. I had visualised a well-laid out meal ready for me at his apartment. I did not sleep that night. I lay awake, wondering how all of it was going to turn out, and what lay ahead. The next morning, I unpacked and made a few calls home. I called Chirag as well. I did not call Saurabh, though. *He is aware of all the details, and yet if he chooses to so horribly step back and come neither to the airport and nor to the hotel, so be it*—I spoke with a firm look of resolution as I stared at the looking glass.

The phone rang and it gave me palpitations. Saurabh's number was flashing on the screen. *Should I take the call? Should I ignore the way he chose to ignore me yesterday and not come to the airport?*

'Hello,' I said.

'Hello, how are you? How was your flight?'

I felt torn apart between the desire to slam the phone down and the yearning to just forget it all and pretend that nothing was amiss. *It is not a big deal that he did not come to the airport, is it?* I did not know what to say. There was an uncomfortable pause that followed.

'You should not have come here, all of a sudden. You never consulted me. Is this how a decent girl ought to behave? How absurd to come down all the way to meet a stranger? Did it strike you that I could be busy and may not have the time to entertain you?' blurted Saurabh curtly.

I was stunned. Nothing could have prepared me for this verbal onslaught from him. I hit the chair with a thud. Saurabh continued to lash out at me, accusing me of harbouring the typical Indian mentality of pursuing rich guys, for the sake of settling abroad. He did not mince words and told me how immature he thought I was.

Tears were streaming down my eyes... The sobs must have escaped my throat though I had tried to quell them. The next instant, he was gently murmuring and telling me to calm down. I could not believe my ears. He was apologising to me, and he sounded genial and pleasing as he did in our online chats. I sat wide-eyed, unable to make any sense of what was happening.

I was confused, and yet decided to put up a brave front. I smiled and we kept on chatting casually about distant subjects. Not a word was said about meeting up, by either one of us.

I took a long, aimless walk in the sprawling Hyde Park near my hotel. When I returned to the hotel, I was too exhausted and upset. I could not sleep that night, as well. All kinds of thoughts were crowding my mind. *What is happening with me? What shall I do now? Why is he behaving so weirdly? He used to be so very affable and seemed to be equally interested in me... Is he scared of commitment, and therefore stepping back or is he trying to intimidate me? Why?*

I tried to come up with all kinds of explanations for his behaviour, but none seemed a plausible one.

The next day, I took some tips from the Help Desk at the hotel and went out to explore the city on my own. I had decided in the wee hours of the morning that since I had spent all my savings for this trip, I was not going to let anyone ruin it. I liked Saurabh while I was chatting with him, but I had no choice if he chose to back out from his rosy promises. I bought a ticket for the Hop On-Hop Off bus tour and spent the entire day, exploring the bewitching sights, seeped in history. It was as if every building and every corner had a glorious past to retell. I was excited and wanted to save and secure every moment in my memory. I marvelled at the Georgian and Victorian architecture and at the sturdy edifices that had seen unbelievable turbulence and destruction many a times; gaped at the numerous multi-cuisine fast-food joints; experimented with delicious ice-cream flavours; and got down at nearly every stop of the bus, explored the place and hopped on once again....

At about 6 pm, my phone rang. It was Saurabh calling and for a moment I hesitated but finally, answered the call. He was polite and asked me how my day was. I decided to sound normal and said the day had been a memorable one. I was afraid that he would ask to meet him, but he spared me the agony of the dilemma it would have posed. He did not ask me any detail about how I had sketched out my trip. I politely thanked him for enquiring on me, and wished him good night.

The sleepless nights were taking a toll; I was unable to think clearly anymore. I was sure that he was deliberately trying to push me away with his disinterested and insolent words. *He is being deliberately rude with me... To hell with him!* I decided to sleep first and then think about what to do only after getting up in the morning.

It was around 10 am when I was awakened by a persistently ringing phone call. I lazily rolled out of the thick covers and looked at my cell phone. It was him again. *Why is he calling*? I took the call half-heartedly.

'Hey, sleepy bird. What are you up to?' Saurabh's voice floated in from the other end.

I was still not sure and muttered, 'Excuse me?'

'Yes, yes... I am talking to you. I have a day off and want to be at your service,' Saurabh offered.

Confusion! 'That is nice of you, Saurabh, but I will explore the city on my own... Don't wish to bother you on your day off.'

'Pleasure is all mine! Come on, get ready... I will be there in half an hour.' And having declared thus, Saurabh disconnected the call.

Reluctantly, I got up and began to get ready—with confusion looming large in my head. I dressed up casually and decided to wait for him in the lobby. The next instant, my heart tugged at me fiercely—urging me to not meet him. Before the mettle could melt,

I called him and politely told him of my desire to not meet him.

'I feel that I do not know you anymore. I am upset at the way you have behaved. I do not wish to meet this graceless new version of you. I thank you for the two phone calls and I wish you the best for your life ahead.'

'You stupid Indian!' he roared into the receiver. 'You just do not know how to talk or behave. What is this supposed to mean? Do you think that like the guys in India, I shall plead and implore you to meet me? I have been trying to cope up with your crazy ways since a fortnight when giggling with excitement, you told me that you have decided to come here. Had it been anyone else, I would have not called even once. Look, I have been trying to be polite with you but you Indian girls—all you do is look for an American or British passport-holder and once you get one, you cannot handle your sheer luck.'

I was aghast at this rant of his. I wanted to stand before him at that moment and slap him with full force or sink in the ground beneath. He was going on as if some unnatural forces had taken hold over him.

The words were piercing the core of my being. Never had I been humiliated thus, in my life. 'You have been on my nerve ever since we started chatting. You Indian girls certainly don't deserve an iota of attention—for you misuse it. Neither are you cultured, and nor do you know how to move ahead with someone who you have just begun talking with. I thought you were a decent girl but I was mistaken.' And while still muttering, he angrily disconnected the line.

I remained numb and in a state of shock all through that day and night. In the wee hours of the morning, I made a cup of tea and sat at the window sill, waiting for dawn to break the darkness of the night. The window offered a beautiful view of the Thames. As I sat sipping the tea, my mind was in a state of turmoil. *Here I am, sitting thousands of miles away from home—all alone and unaware of what this entire episode is supposed to teach me,* I kept thinking. I refused to believe that he did not *like* me. He did, and I knew it. Had I not sensed his emotions, I would have never taken this decision to fly out so far. *Probably, he has some psychological issues and shudders at the prospect of letting someone in his life. This can be a possible explanation for his wayward behaviour,* my instincts were exhorting me. In a flash, I felt as if the mist was cleared.

The next instant, terrifying thoughts gripped me: *What if he had continued to put up an artificial front before me? Had he been sweet all the time, we would have been married in a few months. And, what if his real self would have unfolded before me then?* I sat upright with fright. *Is it not a blessing that his confusions and insecurities and complexes are all out before me before it is too late?* I peered out of the window and looked up at the sky. *Yes, God has been great! Love gave me the wings… I have come to the place I always wanted to and am living my dream.*

I liked him, and I stepped forth. Probably, he liked me too and hence, he is stepping back, I told myself wryly, as the first ray of the dawn pierced the beautiful skyline of London.

'How Dare You?'

I returned from London with feelings such as joy, exhilaration and disappointment-laced relief—all mixed and intertwined in my mind. In the search for a groom, an innate desire of mine had been fulfilled. I had bathed in the nectar of beauty and tranquillity as I spent some lovely hours walking for miles and miles. I had hitherto just read the lines penned by Wordsworth: *I wander'd lonely as a cloud*, but in the moments I was there, I could feel and live the emotions he must have felt for it is the quintessential Lake District poem. I was held spellbound by the majestic mountains and breathtakingly delightful lakes. Even if the encounter with Saurabh had left me misty-eyed and bitter in the mouth, the thrills during the rest of the days in Windermere and Grasmere and the gleeful people I met in the homestays and the tour guides who guided me—had made the entire experience an incredible one. I returned home, cool and happy.

And yet, there were moments I felt extremely irritable. However, every time I recollected what had transpired on the phone in London and how things could have all gone horribly worse had I moved forward with Saurabh, I felt extremely restless. Immediately on returning, I had told Chirag of all that had transpired there. He had been shocked, sympathetic and finally, relieved. Yet, I had not succeeded in taking it all out of my system. *Does anything of this sort happen with others too? Or, am I the only chosen one?*

Feelings of irritability swooped over me so very strongly on some days that I ended up sending a tear-stained face emoji to Chirag on WhatsApp.

Me: 'Hello ☹'

Chirag: 'Hey, Leena. What happened? This face is not you!'

Me: 'Well, whenever there is a choice between smiling and whining, there are times I choose whining, and particularly so with those one doesn't need to pretend with… Am I wrong? Must I always think of how you or some other pal wants to see me as and behave accordingly?'

Chirag: 'Relax, Leena. You seem to be upset. Let's chat another time.'

Me: 'Why? Why should we choose time and words which are always smooth and convenient? Let us talk now….'

Chirag: 'I know, Leena that things did not go well with Saurabh in London but, hey…cheer up! Appreciate the brighter side of your trip. You did some amazing things in London. You yourself told me and sounded so cool the other day. Why is there the need to pity yourself then?'

Me: 'You know what… I know you are a wise guy who seems to know and understand it all. But there are things even you would not understand. I agree that I end up confiding pretty much everything but then you do not have to pet and pat me every time. One cannot always look up at the brighter side every time. It is not human. And by the way, I do not pity myself. I pity the fact that people do not know as to how much they disappoint. Their secrets…their waywardness…their eccentricities—all of it hurts.'

A long pause ensued….

Chirag: 'Yes! Saurabh should not have held back this way. He should have come out clean with what lay inside of him.'

Me: 'Have you?'

Chirag: 'What do you mean?'

He was obviously taken aback. But the fact was that there was quite a lot I did not know about him, as well. *So, perhaps all guys walked about with their closets safeguarded and skeletons inside.*

Me: 'I do not think I said anything which was difficult to grasp. I plainly asked if you have been transparent yourself. Isn't there a lot that I do not know about you? Why the heck do all guys have to be cryptographers, while we break our heads in trying to decode your apparent and underlying messages?'

I stomped my foot under the study table and even kicked it hard on both the sides. Of course, I winced in pain the next moment!

Another long pause followed.

Chirag: 'I think you know almost everything about me. And right now, is this chat about me or you?'

Me: 'That is exactly the point! Why do all of our chats and talks have to be about me? Why is all the divulging from one end? And yes, there is much I do know about you. Haven't you carefully evaded talking about your personal life? Do you have a wife? Are you single? How many children do you have? I do not know even if right now you are in a relationship....'

This time, the pause is awkward.

Chirag: 'There is nothing to tell. I don't feel comfortable talking about my personal life right now.'

Me (inserting a few eye-roll emojis): 'Oh, well....'

Chirag: 'Why do you have to use that mocking tone? Should two people weigh exactly as to who is sharing how much in a friendship? Why this curiosity to know about my wife and kids?'

Me: 'Aha...there is someone, for sure. A pretty wife perhaps or a girlfriend? High on the socioprofessional ladder? Just like you…at least, tell me if you have kids? How many and how old? Where do your parents live? With you, or in India?'

Chirag: 'Hey, hey, hey! Enough! I know I should have told you a bit about my personal life. But, I am not up to it… I must go now. Let's talk later.'

Me: 'But, why? Why can't you just share? As I do…'

Chirag: 'Fine! If you wish to not share with me, because I haven't—it is alright. Stop sharing with me… I must go now. Take care.'

Me: 'Yes, I shall stop it. Nothing, from now onwards… Goodbye.'

Chirag: 'Bye. Let's talk after you have calmed down.'

I banged my fists hard on the table this time.

Thirty seconds later, Mom shouted from the kitchen, 'Leena, have some mercy on your study table. The one with whom you were chatting cannot even see your anguish. And, what is the use of yoga when the teacher herself has to bang tables! If not to me, at least show some respect to the table!'

Exasperated, I shouted back, 'Okay!'

A few minutes later, Mom peeked from the door and said, lovingly, 'I know you should not be eating these fried things but the *palak* was so fresh and Shaurya insisted on having *palak-puris* in the evening. Come and have them piping hot. You shall feel better.'

To my utter relief, Mom had no clue of the entire Saurabh episode. Of course, her outbursts about my refusal to take deep and serious strides in the direction of matrimony did take place with amazing and awe-inspiring regularity so much so that very often no external prod was needed to stimulate the nerves. Her monologues carried the same tone, spirit, and subject. A few samplers being:

'You must be scaring them off with your stupid ideologies.'

'You say *No* to a guy who lives in a joint family; you say *No* to the probability of kids after marriage; and on top of it—you are an atheist... Why do you not listen to me for once and come to take the blessings of Swami Dilbhara*ji*? Who knows, there might be an issue with the stars and the planets. He can see them all with his naked eyes and knows to put them in their right place, as well.'

'Oh God, you are the only one I have faith in! Only you can do something. Why did you choose me to see such days and give me such *extraaaa-ordinary* kids?'

'Binnie, I am sure you come across as too intimidating for the poor menfolk.'

One look at Mom the very next morning and I knew instinctively that I was to be smoothly rounded up with a satirical admonition. I cautiously tiptoed into the kitchen and sat in the chair, intending to gulp down a cup of tea and make a fastidious escape. It started with a sharp hiss of her in-drawn breath and then the customary clink…clank…and clatter of the vessels, followed by the inaudible murmurs to begin with. I could see what was to follow. Surely, one of her friends must have messaged her early in the morning about some development, the sparks of which were going to engulf me into flames shortly. I did not have to wait for more than two minutes.

'I had told you, don't go to Bengaluru, but why would you listen? You had decided to go; you just packed your bags and scooted! And then, after returning from there, you once again packed your bags and off you went to London too! Who behaves like that? Can't think of any daughters of any of my friends who are capable of such dumbness! Now, just see, we are still standing from where we started. Kanta Mehta's daughter—the one who is a divorcee got remarried when you were away and her mother called this morning to tell that she is expecting a baby. I could see through the telephone that Mrs Mehta was making faces and smiling maliciously at me.'

My Mom had quite a *vision,* didn't she? People heard through phones, but she could see through them! I listened to the verbal tirades with a customised (acquired with quite a lot of practice) blank look on the face. Sometimes, I hugged her lovingly during such a spree and then she calmed down… I was not sure what to do this time. *Should I argue or fight back? Or just plainly put my foot down for once and declare that I will do as I please? Or should I just meekly apologise?* I had to say something….

'Mom, I know I disappoint you. I listen to my heart far too often and end up hurting you as well as myself in the process. Though I am deeply confused about why exactly do I wish to get remarried, I am still trying to do as you say, Mom. I do not know if I am scared of my ageing or of ending up alone at the end or if I shall stay happily in my own company. Since I am confused, I decided to listen to what you felt was the right thing for me. I meet guys whom either you suggest from the portal or some whom I bump into in the hope that I shall find someone worthy of living together. But yes, I am still confused, Mom. And that is why it sometimes gets a little too much for me and then I try to wriggle out of this entire mishmash.'

There were two pairs of moist eyes then and there. She squeezed my hand warmly and I hugged her one more time. This time, for a little while longer.

Later in the day, I was sitting in the college staff room, surfing my mailbox, waiting for the bell to ring and the next lecture to resume. I suddenly recollected how nasty I had been with Chirag the previous day. I decided to apologise to him.

To: chiragevohra@gmail.com

Sub: I am sorry

Hello Chirag,

Where do I begin? I am feeling embarrassed at my stupid behaviour the other day. I was, of course, not in my senses. The episode with Saurabh has taken its toll on my sanity… Will you please forgive and forget that chat? Can we talk sometime?

Leena

Email Sent.

Inbox (1)

To: leena.yoga@gmail.com

Sub: Re: I am sorry

Hey Leena,

We are good. Let's talk soon. I won't be available for the next few weeks. Travelling for work. Write to me if there is anything.

Cheers!

Chirag

Close on the heels of Chirag's email, Mom's mail popped up in the Inbox: 'Here, take a look at this profile.

He is a Financial Analyst and settled in your favourite country—Singapore. He is just tailor-made for you, Binnie. He is a travel freak like you, and seems to be a foodie too!'

A faint ray of hope fell upon my jarred and scarred mind once again. I clicked at the profile. *Hmm, let me see... Am I ready for another laddoo? Hmm...guess I am! His name is—Sanjay Mirchandani. Okay, let me enlarge his profile picture. Aha! He looks decent!*

The information given was: 'Hi, I am putting up this profile on behalf of my son. He is a Singapore resident, hailing from Delhi; alma mater: DPS; is a financial analyst; owns a start-up and a condo with a sea view in Singapore. His friends describe him as affectionate, caring, creative, easy-going, modest and respectful. His parents, that is, we have our own business in Delhi. My son's ideal partner should be responsible, caring and compassionate, educated and a homely girl who enjoys time with family and friends, and loves good food and travel.'

Okay, uncle ji. Got it! Too much bragging about one's son and too many expectations from the superwoman you seek as his bride... Typical indeed!

I messaged Mom: 'This Sanjay guy can't even create his own profile, Mom! I don't think he has time to get married. His father is operating on his behalf. He is a financial analyst and these people don't even have time to breathe and that's how they own condos with a sea view in Singapore.'

Mom replied: 'Poor guy, must be working hard and cannot find time. How does that not make him eligible? And, why do you have an issue if the father cares… Don't criticise this *Beeba* Boy. Have I not created your profile? Does that alter who you are or your sincere intent?'

Me: 'Fine, I take your point. By the way, the profile is good.'

Sanjay Mirchandani—Marwari or Sindhi? I wondered.

I mailed him: Hi

He replied: I like your profile, Leena. Let us talk!

I replied: Hey Sanjay, nice to connect. Let us chat sometime. Have to go to take a class now….

My readiness (minus the usual fuss) to communicate with the *laddoo* suggested by Mom, made our dinner-table conversation sweeter that night. Mom had a mischievous smile on her face. I felt relieved.

At around 10 pm, I was almost about to curl and snuggle down in my blanket, when my WhatsApp notification buzzed. *Who could it be at this hour?* I looked at the message which came from a number in Singapore (+65…): 'Hey Leena, this is Sanjay. I just got online and buzzed. Your mother was online too and we briefly spoke. She passed your number. Is it okay to talk now?'

Mommmmmmm! I wanted to scream.

Me: 'Hey Sanjay, errr... It is a little late but yes, a quick chat won't hurt. How are you?'

Sanjay: 'I am good. How about you?'

Me: 'I am very well.'

Sanjay: 'I am not sure if I ought to have buzzed privately, so soon.'

Me: 'No, no...that is okay!' (I smiled at this display of chivalry.)

Sanjay: 'Leena, I happened to read some of the stuff you have written on blogs and a few web-portals. I also read one of your articles in which you have shared some interesting insights on the meaning of life. I liked the simplicity with which you have described the little joys of life which we tend to overlook in the hustle and bustle of our daily living. Here in Singapore, everything and everyone is just so flamboyant! It is often a struggle to find the genuine side of people; to find their genuine expressions. Guess, the lifestyle here is such... Maybe that is why I found your profile so very striking.'

He seems to be one of those thinking types... I found myself wide awake and wanting to listen to more from him. Had I looked at myself in the mirror just then, I would have seen a happy face with a broad, ear-to-ear grin.

What had begun as a quick chat eventually lasted for over an hour. From Singapore to India; from DPS to St. Mary's School; and from *momos* of Singapore to the *chole-bhature* at Chanakyapuri—everything was discussed amidst bouts of laughter and amazement.

Me: 'Hey Sanjay, isn't it almost the middle of the night at your end?'

Sanjay: 'Ah, yes! I did not realise that it is almost time for the dawn to break. You are such a terrific conversationalist, Leena. No wonder, you are a lecturer. I am sure the students are enraptured listening to you way past the lecture hours. Would you like to do a video-chat on Sunday? Let me show you my condo and we can talk more about the books we love to read. What say?'

The looking glass would have then, at that instant, seen a face going crimson red... I found myself blushing and replied, 'Sounds like a plan to me, Sanjay!'

The next two days simply whizzed past trying to meet deadlines at work, completing the pending chores at home and of course, in feeling excited about seeing Sanjay on Sunday. A few *'Hey, how is it going?'*

messages were exchanged in those two days. I did not want to get too excited, but then I felt certain that we had hit it off on a positive note.

I knew Mom had to go for her weekly potluck lunch on Sunday with her friends and I smartly picked up that time when I would be able to comfortably chat with Sanjay. Though Papa was at home, he was a darling who never intruded, remained immersed in his own world and happily so, particularly when Mom was in absentia. That morning, I took extra efforts at cleaning my room. I changed the bed covers, re-arranged the books so as to make the scholarly and spiritual ones visible in the front row, placed a few indoor plants, wore a nice Punjabi-suit and waited for the call. We had already exchanged our Skype IDs, the previous night.

At about 1 pm, Mom left and right after her departure, I could hear the Skype call alert.

Oh yes, it is him... I shot one last look at myself in the mirror and took the call.

Sanjay appeared on my 14-inch computer screen. He looked dapper in a pink shirt; he was fair and had a glorious mane of neatly styled hair... His smile was infectious; it could make a girl's heart skip a beat.

I nudged myself out of my daydream and returned the smile.

'Hello, Leena, it is nice to be able to see you. Am I on time?'

Yes, indeed! My heart was pounding so very loudly that I could not even hear my own reply.

'It is a strange feeling—for I have never spoken with anyone so soon. I feel a bit shy.'

An awkward silence ensued, which I broke finally. 'What is that striking painting behind you, Sanjay?'

'I like collecting paintings. I bought this one from an art exhibition which I attended last week. This is an abstract by one of my favourite artists.'

He is a connoisseur of art! I almost exclaimed. This was all looking too good to be true.

'Let me show you around the house,' he offered.

For the next ten minutes, I took a sneak peek into Sanjay's expensively set up condo by the sea side. It had just the right proportion of furniture, books, decorative artefacts and utilities. The sea view from his living room was simply spectacular! I was floored, at the end of it.

'Leena, I was earlier in the US and now have been in Singapore for about five years but, I intend to move around to a new place every three to five years if opportunities come my way. Are you fine with that?'

Oh my God! This must be a dream, I told myself. I wanted to shout: *Yesssssssss, I love the idea of moving to places and seeing distinct cultures and trying cuisines and....*

I was tongue-tied and just managed to nod amiably.

'Wow, that is great! Hey, will you please give me five minutes? I need to offload my washed clothes and put them in the dryer.'

Oh God! Please pinch me if this is a dream... Ah, he is different! Someone who would surely share the load!

'Did you like my place, Leena?'

'Of course, I loved it. Should I show you my little den?'

'I would love to see... I want to know if your room is as charming as you are, Leena.'

I virtually took him around my neatly decorated room and I could see a look of admiration in his eyes.

'Your room is indeed beautiful and speaks volumes about your personality.'

A question had been pricking my mind for a long time. I decided to shoot it across. 'Sanjay, tell me, what made you decide to take a plunge into matrimony once again?'

'You have posed a good question. You see, I have been living all by myself for the past three years.

I am earning well, my future growth prospects are bright and my family is quite supportive of my achievements and decisions. I think I am ready to settle down again. I visit my family in Delhi every six months but it still does get lonely here sometimes. And especially when your friends always move about with their partners—for movies, parties, barbeques, you…you get this feeling of being the "odd man out".'

The pounding of the heart slowed down a bit and my brain took over the gears. 'Okay, and…?'

'See, Leena, I am basically very happy with my company. In fact, I love myself but when it comes to hanging out with friends, I feel like a loser because they are all married and their lives revolve around their respective wives and kids. I don't want to lose them. I want to hang around and be in the same circle.'

The vagaries of the heart were receding and the floodlights of reality were swarming over…. All of a sudden, the colours in the abstract painting behind Sanjay began to make my eyes sore. *The colours are too morose,* I thought. And yet, the heart refused to give up the reins altogether. It needed further clarification before taking a bow.

'Please, correct me if I am assuming incorrectly. You want to get married in order to be accepted by your married friends and seen as one of the inner circle? You wish to have fun along with your married friends and not be left out? This is why you want to settle again?' I spelled it out.

'No, you don't get it, Leena. When you are with someone, you are more readily accepted. When you go to parties, you are considered an insider and one can participate in the spouse-related-gossip sessions... One is considered as one of the brethren; as an equal. You get the invites easily, if one has a pretty face to arrive with. Moreover, you no longer have to come home to coleslaw and baked beans from work...for someone would have cooked at home!'

Yes, right! Someone will be home to cook your food, wash your clothes and then dress up to be pompously flaunted around in your married friends' circle!

Of course, I did not say all or any of the above to Sanjay. I thought for several moments and looked up at him in the camera. His infectious smile was still intact but it was no longer making the butterflies flutter in my stomach.

'Sanjay, do you want to marry to find a friend to talk to, to share and be your significant other? Or do you want to marry to impress others? Are you fearful of being left out? Is this why you wish to marry?'

'What do you mean, Leena?'

I could see the smile shrinking gradually… He had even raised his eyebrows, and then he no longer looked irresistible. 'Sanjay, do you really want to get married for yourself?'

'Of course, I want to get married.' The volume of his voice was rising and his tone, changing….

I patiently began, 'Let me ask again… Do you wish to get married for yourself? Or, do you just need a trophy-wife to impress your friends? I do not honestly think that you want a companion for yourself; you instead need a gate-pass so that you can have access to parties and peer groups.'

The smile on his face had left him altogether by the time I spoke my heart out. His eyebrows were further raised and nostrils looked red and flared.

'How dare you? Rubbish! You are talking frivolous! How the hell can you ask me such a stupid thing? I wish to marry and that is why I am here, talking to you patiently; that is why I am on that idiotic matrimonial website; and that is why I cancelled my plan to go for a movie with my friends, who along with their wives and kids must be sitting in a plush theatre, having a great time! What a fool have I been! I decided to sit here and waste my time talking to you, and listening to your nonsense. You have wasted my time. I will no longer continue with this dumb discussion.'

And he disconnected.

It took me a couple of seconds to realise that I was no longer on a video-chat. I sat stunned for quite a while, until a shrill voice rang out in my ears.

'Good that he gave us a glimpse of his temperament. We have been saved from getting into a disaster. Forget him! He needs a full-time assistant and a part-time escort. Let us continue scanning some more profiles. By the way, I came back early because everybody there was discussing Alia's latest release. I thought you are at home and we can go together. Will you book the tickets online or shall we just go directly to the theatre?'

Mom was standing at the door of my bedroom, with an affectionate *let-us-ignore-the-idiots* look on her face.

The Bengalurean Madrasi

'By three methods we may learn wisdom. First, by reflection, which is the noblest; second, by imitation, which is the easiest; and third, by experience, which is the bitterest'—the words of Confucius are saved on the screen of my laptop.

Chirag had sent me the wise quote after I had divulged to him the details of my failed marriage. I was staring at the quote, trying to pacify myself. My mind was seething with anguish; I was unsure whether I was more hurt at my own foolish eagerness to chat with just about anyone or whether this dull-headed Sanjay made me sick.

The heaviness in my heart was getting too much to bear. I looked up at the watch and instinctively called up Chirag. After a brief exchange of pleasantries, and without politely asking him if he was busy or free to talk for a while, I unloaded myself.

'Chirag, just tell me honestly… Is there something seriously wrong with me that I end up attracting all smarty-pants in my life? I am sick of them all… Just because I have registered on an online portal and decided to give myself a second chance in marriage, the whole world seems to have conspired to make me go through shit.'

'Hey, hey! Slow down, dearie... What has happened? Why have you raised banners against poor guys?'

I found myself almost blushing on hearing *dearie* from the other end. *No Leena, no silly ideas popping in your head now and complicating matters further.* I recounted Sanjay's call to Chirag. As I repeated what he had said before slamming the phone down, I felt worse than I had in the afternoon.

And yet, I sensed that Chirag was barely suppressing his chuckles. But he smartly held himself back and just about stopped coming in my line of fire.

'Believe me, Leena, I am trying to get angry at it all but I find myself amused instead. I am so sorry that you are going through all of this... I know that every time it is not easy for you to step into unknown waters. But unless, we dip our toes to test and check thoroughly, how would we know who is to be ticked off? Treat all of these experiences a little dispassionately, for they are going to be there only for a short time and only until you finally tick on somebody.'

'I know that, Chirag and I understand it all and that is why I brace myself before every such dip but....'

'It is never easy to become wiser without becoming a little cynical or bitter. It needs an uncanny ability to have that amused, spectator kind of an attitude. Okay, now let us put this Sanjay aside and tell me what are you reading these days?'

I felt a little better and a lot lighter in the days that followed.

I tried to build on the coveted spectator attitude, during my long walks and meditative moments in the early mornings.

Life is not too bad; it is largely intriguing and sometimes incredible too—thus I summed up Life to myself. One could smile and get on with life pretty much easily, if one willed to. I got over the not-so-good moments and made a coffee-table book of my visit to the United Kingdom and showcased it as an important masterpiece in my living room with pride.

One fine day, as I was getting ready to go to college, I got a call from a former colleague, Arun. He once worked in our college's IT department. I was pleasantly surprised to hear from him.

'Hey Arun, how are you? Oh my God, it's been a long time. Have you been dead?'

'Ha ha! I am very much alive. You know I am a tech-addict. I was busy developing an App and am now a proud owner of that App. I have started my own company and there are about fifteen people in my team,' Arun replied in an upbeat manner.

'Wonderful! That is great! Yes, yes… It is no surprise to know that you too have been swept off by the wave of entrepreneurship. I am happy for you. This calls for a treat!'

'Of course, a treat is due and it shall be soon. For now, I need your help.'

'Tell me.'

'Well, I have developed a dating App and we have about 2,000 registered users so far. I am in the process of scaling it up and reaching out to a few trusted friends to get on to the App, try it and tell me how to make it better and bigger.'

'So?'

'You are one of the smartest women I know! And, I guess, single too, aren't you? Plus, you have always been a supportive friend. Please try it.'

'Who? Me? No, no… I can't. Yes, I am presently single. But I won't do all this stuff. Please excuse me, Arun.'

'Hey, hey…hear me out, please. My App is not just another run-of-the-mill one. We have a lot of screening steps before we take someone on our list and match two people based on at least 8–10 common traits. Come on, Leena. I know you are among those who will actually give me a genuine feedback and what more, you may find someone interesting. Please, please....'

He was so persistent, that I had to submit. Reluctantly, I agreed and stored the details of the dating App in order to check it out later. In my mind, I was clear—*later* meant *never*. The mere thought of looking at one more *laddoo* sent a shiver down my spine.

But one's friends are often one's mirror images. If I was stubborn, he was even more so. Arun was so relentless with his requests that every other day, he kept reminding me to log on. Finally, on a Sunday morning after gobbling down a yummy brunch made by Mom which had elevated my mood, I scrolled up Arun's messages on how to download the App and get started.

As soon as I logged in, I received a message: 'Welcome to *Single-Mingle,* Leena. We have authenticated your identity. Please set your preferences, and post your picture along with a brief profile so as to let the single men out there know you as a person. Do you need a Tip?'

No, thanks, I muttered to myself and uploaded a brief note, along with a picture of myself flashing my vivacious smile. The App required me to also fill columns mentioning my interests, funny/interesting moments and the reasons for being there on the App. To the latter question, I wanted to reply—*Arun pestered me to be here, and so here I am.* However, I solemnly wrote: 'To connect with like-minded people.'

And then the App paired me up with about twenty-five strangers in one shot. Bingo!

One message: 'Hey your smile is cute.'

I ignored it.

Another message: 'Hey Leena, nice name.'

I ignored it too.

One more message: 'What brings you here, Leena?'

I wanted to snap back: *Can't you read it on my profile?* Of course, I ignored it.

Twenty unread messages popped up. I ignored them all.

Forty unread messages... I kept ignoring.

I was tucked in bed around 9 pm when another buzz made me instinctively pick up my phone lying on the bed-side table.

The message read: 'Hey Leena, this is Raghav here. Happened to stumble upon your profile, and wanted to say hello. I am a tech-founder, a divorcee, crazy about kick-boxing with my son to keep myself fit and when not in office, I can be found in the kitchen trying out new recipes. It will be nice to get connected with a lecturer who also happens to have a sweet smile.'

I hesitated a bit but decided to reply.

Me: 'Hi, Raghav. It will be nice to connect.'

Raghav: 'Hey, I appreciate the prompt reply. Don't the teachers sleep early?'

Me: 'Yes, they do.'

Raghav: 'Then, what is keeping you awake today?'

Me: 'Well, I lazed for more than the usual hours today… Hence, not sleepy.'

Raghav: 'Sounds cool… Hey, what is it like to be a teacher; a facilitator of change? You are into moulding mankind; shaping the future of our society.'

Raghav's simple and witty remark made me laugh out loud.

Me: 'Thank you, for a quick laughter therapy before sleep. Oh, it is nothing of that sort. I am simply following my passion and passing on this passion to others, who happen to meet me on this journey. I feel fortunate to be able to do what I think I do well.'

Raghav: 'Super… I like that. By the way, Madam Leena—would you care for some gnocchi? I just made it.'

Me: 'Wow, what is that? I have heard of it, but never tried making it myself.'

Raghav: 'It is an Italian dish made with flour, eggs and potatoes. Only takes a few minutes to prepare, and is served with a rich tomato sauce, which of course has also been made by this tech-head.'

Me: 'Hmm… Interesting! So, you have a son. How old is he?'

Raghav: 'My son is eight now, and is extremely naughty, though quite helpful in the kitchen. He does the chopping, while I do the cooking and garnishing. He goes to a day-school here, in Bengaluru.'

Me: 'Very nice… Not many parents encourage kids in the kitchen. You seem to have fewer hassles.'

Raghav: 'Thanks… I gotta go now before the gnocchi gets cold and my son's temper gets hot. Let's stay in touch. Bye.'

Me: 'Yes, let us stay in touch. Bye.'

There was something striking about Raghav which kept me awake for quite a while. I made an extra effort to go through his profile once again. *His looks were average*; height, medium; complexion, dark, and face, typically South Indian. I even looked up the net and found a few videos of him lecturing young techies at various summits and symposia. *Hmm… Interesting…* I mumbled sleepily and dozed off.

I was busy over the next week and almost forgot about Raghav and the dating App. It was not until Sunday evening that my *Single-Mingle* mailbox flashed his message.

Raghav: 'Hello, Ms Lecturer! How have you been?'

Me: 'Oh, it's you, Raghav! I am fine, you say....'

Raghav: 'A charming lady never buzzed. So I thought, why be an egoist? Let me do the needful. Hope I am not bothering you too much.'

Me: 'No... It's just that the week was busy. What is happening at your end?'

Raghav: 'Well, I had travelled to Delhi for work and on returning the kiddo's weekend exam kept me busy.'

Me: 'Oh, you were in Delhi? Why did you not call? We could have met over coffee.'

As soon as I said the last line, I wanted to retract it. *It is none of my business as to where he goes or comes and whom he calls or does not call,* I rebuked myself.

Me: 'Oops, am so sorry... Errr, I should not have asked you that.'

Raghav: 'Seriously, I wanted to call you too, Leena but I was a bit hesitant. We have barely connected. It would have been quite a rush.'

Me: 'Hmm, I do understand. So, what did you do in Delhi?'

Raghav: 'Well, after the usual work-related meetings, I caught up with a few old friends. In fact, this friend of mine, Arun, was insistent that I meet him because he wants me to mentor him.'

Me: 'Arun?!?!'

Raghav: 'Yes, Arun. Why? You sound surprised?'

Me: 'Is this friend of yours—Arun, by any chance, a techie like you are and also someone who owns this App?'

I waited for his reply with bated breath.

Raghav: 'You are scaring me now. Yes, he is!'

Me: 'Oh my God! We live in a small world, indeed! He is my friend too. We worked together until a few years ago.'

Raghav: 'Oh... Okay, wait a second! Leena, please do not tell me you are here because Arun almost begged you, is it?'

After a pause, I nodded my head in affirmation along with typing a 'Yes' in the chat box.

Raghav: 'Holy crap! I too am a tester for this App and met Arun to suggest how to improvise on the user experience.'

For the next few seconds, Raghav and I simply exchanged the Ha! Ha! Ha!-type emoticons.

The chat continued and we came to know each other's interests, passions and a little bit about how our lives had shaped up so far. It was interesting to know that Raghav belied the median Tamil Brahmin who is rarely adventurous or conspicuously unorthodox. He came across as competent, but not conventional and conformist. He kept me drawn by sharing his cross-cultural encounters with people from across the country and even from over half the world. I looked at the watch and was astonished to see the hours that had flown by.

Me: 'Hey, it is almost midnight. I got to go to the college tomorrow.'

Raghav: 'Yes, I realise I blabbered too much, sorry.'

Me: 'Oh no, not at all... It is fine. I was happily listening. Good night.'

Raghav: 'Good night. Tomorrow, you share your encounters and stories.'

Me: 'Okay, sure... Done.'

After logging out, I was kind of convinced that trying out the dating App was perhaps not a bad idea, after all!

I mumbled a *Thank you, Arun* before falling asleep.

The next couple of months saw us increasing the frequency of our chats, in addition to the occasional phone calls. We gained further insights into each other's lives. At the same time, I was treading cautiously and also taking it easy. I let each day and every conversation with him to unfold on its own. I had begun enjoying his company and was happy to find a mature, witty and a sincere friend in Raghav.

Another Sunday dawned and before it could inflict some nonsense on me, I decided to very well waste it. *What are some of the silliest things I can possibly do? Let me see… Oh yes! Taaaa daaaaaa… Will ask Mom to recommend the spiciest saas-bahu soap and then ask her to oil my hair and then I can file my nails, apply a mask and, also update my Facebook page.* I was satisfied. There could not be a sillier day spent.

I decided to start with going to my Facebook page. It had been so long that I could not remember my password. *What was my password? pgwodehouse? ekomkar? No… No… Umm… Oh, yes… fir-se-single!*

I logged in. It had been months. It was overloaded with notifications, friend recommendations, friend requests, lame pictures of my friends vacationing in different corners of the world; some had atrociously clicked and posted 'attending my best friend's wedding' selfies, while others bragged about their respective *makeovers* or about how the wise words of some self-styled life coach had overhauled them. I am so sure that everyone who is on Facebook, pursues relentlessly a single-point agenda and that is: to make the others who are on the site question their own boring, mundane, meaningless and glamour-less existences on this planet! Everybody wants to convince everyone else on it that his or her life is anything but crap!

As I scrolled through suggestions to be friends from Facebook experts, I paused at a name: Tara Jain, California.

I was naturally curious. I clicked on her profile. It read: A lover of life, an Architect in her mid-30s and a loving 'pal' to all her lovely friends, Tara….

Halfway through her profile, I began to peer closely at her photo and found her very elegant and stylish. She seemed to be in total charge of herself. Her eyes were almond-shaped and held a deep gaze. I scrolled down.

Tara had posted a photo (a group of people holding hands together and sitting in a circle) a week ago which was captioned: *'Happy meditative moments with friends who "care" and a special friend for whom I "care".'*

In another photo, she was smiling coyly and leaning on a guy's shoulder.

As I was about to move on to other posts, my eyes caught the sight of the guy whose shoulders were being put to some good use. I gasped. *Heavens! No! This just cannot be! It is Chirag! I zoomed in the image… Yes, this is Chirag. Both are beaming in the photo. Is she Chirag's wife? Girlfriend? Who is she calling her 'special friend'? She is so pretty. They look engrossed... In meditation or in each other?*

I impatiently scrolled down hoping to see (or, hoping not to?) more connections between Chirag and this woman. But there was nothing further I could lay eyes on, which concerned me. There were no juicy titbits to suggest anything of consequence.

Just then, Mom's voice rang out shrill from the next room.

'Binnie dear, you are online, aren't you on Facebook? Thank God! I was worried that you had probably blocked my profile, but of course, you would never dream of doing that. We are not just mother and daughter; we are buddies!'

I looked towards the door, anticipating her barging in any moment. *Should I hunt further about Tara? Perhaps, later....*

'Binnie, can you please share the picture I just uploaded of our Manali trip? I have captioned it: *Move aside Kareena and Malaika... We are the new #BFFs in town... Mother-daughter Duo. #YoManali*. Cool, isn't it? There shall be a shower of *likes*. You just see... My friends are going to gush over our camaraderie.'

My mind was in an iffy. Amongst the plethora of thoughts and doubts, this Tara too had now barged in and was adding to the congestion.

'Mom, can you please leave me alone for some time? I am busy.' I sighed.

'I knew it. How can you break your record of never heeding to what I say at the first instant! No! I think you are embarrassed of letting people know that you are *friends* with your own mother on Facebook.'

'Mommmm, do you have to…?'

She had entered the room, sniffing and wiping her nose with a tissue. She sat down on the bed. I sighed.

'*Beta*, should I have any hopes from you in my old age when you can't even share a picture with me on your Facebook page. Is that too much to expect from one's own daughter? Tell me, today. Once and for all… Are you ashamed to be seen with me?'

The sniffing intensified.

'FIIINEEE! Here, I just shared our photo on my page with two hearts under it.'

Mom had that typical look of triumph. 'Binnie dear, will you please repeat the hashtags on your profile as well? It just makes us more searchable.'

'Yes, okay.' I copy-pasted the hashtags and knew that a diversion was imperative.

'Mom, should I make ginger-lemon tea for you? You must be so tired….'

The rest of the day, I could not focus on either my nails or on the nymphs on Mom's favourite soap.

At about 5 pm, a message flashed on the cell. I was surprised to see Raghav writing 'Hi'.

Me: 'Hey Raghav, today is Sunday. Isn't it your day with the kiddo? On Sundays, we usually chat at night, isn't it?'

Raghav: 'Yes, yes... We are spending our Sunday together. Just finished a swimming session and Suraj is still in the pool. I called to let you know that an urgent meeting with a client has been scheduled in Delhi tomorrow. I will be in your city for two days and have a return flight to Bengaluru on Tuesday night. Would Madam care for a dinner at a restaurant tomorrow night with me?'

Me: 'Certainly... Wow! Let's meet.'

Raghav: 'Great! I will connect with you tomorrow afternoon and we shall make a plan. I have a fair idea of most of the places in Delhi and of course, Google maps will rescue me in case you choose your favourite place which I haven't been to.'

Me: 'Sure... See you tomorrow.'

I was chirpier than usual, the next day. I even smiled at my Mom's gossip updates and did not forget to tell her that I was going to go out for dinner. Mom too was so busy trying out a new recipe of *kathi rolls* that she did not enquire much about my dinner date.

The day rolled by, and I returned home, got ready for the evening and as planned, left home at 7 pm. Raghav had already called me twice to fix the time and re-confirm the location of the restaurant, which I had chosen as it happened to be one of my favourites.

I reached on time—sharp at 7.30 pm and found Raghav already seated in a corner. As I approached him, I noticed that he certainly did not look his age (42 years); he looked much younger. There was an innocent boyish charm on his dark-brown face and yet he seemed well-poised and completely at ease. *But hey, strange...why are his lips unusually dark? Never mind... He looks better in real than on his profile picture!* I hesitated for an instant but then made a stride in his direction.

'Madam Leena! A pleasure to finally meet you,' said Raghav as he stood up to shake hands with me.

'Likewise, Raghav. By the way, I am happy to see that you are on time,' I complemented in return.

'It is one of the cherished principles of my life—to value time! Now, may we order first and then continue? I am famished.'

At first, we ordered vegetarian appetisers and mocktails and started chatting. Raghav seemed to be smitten by something about me, and it was not hard to guess. He later admitted that he was transfixed by my smile. He was a smart conversationalist, and kept me enthused with his wit and sense of humour. His mature side was revealed when he spoke fondly about his relationship with his son. Not once did he ask or expect me to reciprocate. His carefree mannerisms and the relaxed air that he had about him appealed to me the most. There was not an iota of pressure or any kind of heaviness while being with and chatting with him.

After dinner, I did not mind a stroll to a bistro with him which was just a few steps away. It was getting late but I had already messaged Mom and so far, things were going smoothly.

Suddenly, Raghav stopped walking and looking up towards me, asked: 'Leena, if you will excuse me, I need a smoke. Is it okay if you go ahead and I join you in five minutes?'

Though I did mind that, I simply nodded and walked alone towards the bistro. *Oh, this is the reason for his darkened lips,* I now knew. I had just about settled down when within a few minutes, Raghav showed up. We ordered two cappuccinos.

A silence hung in the air until Raghav spoke. 'I am a smoker. It so happened that after the divorce which I was not the least prepared for, the responsibility of single-handedly parenting a child was thrust on me, and coupled with the pressures of making headway in my career, I took to smoking. It was once a necessity for me. Been ten years into it but now I have decided to gradually reduce and eventually quit. It will not be easy but I have been through harder times in life. My wife left us—me and Suraj—when he was barely six months old. We were in the United States at that time and I was at the peak of my career. It hit me out of the blue when one day, I came home to find a handwritten note from her saying, "I am leaving, Raghav. I cannot compromise with my career, which I am afraid I will have to, now that we have a child. I feel the mistake was mutual but I cannot put the rest of my life at stake now. I know you will be a good father. Goodbye!"'

The earnestness with which he spoke, left me teary-eyed. *Poor guy, how much has he endured, and yet he is so easy-going....*

He continued, 'Leena, it was not easy for me at all. All of a sudden, I was completely and wholly responsible for managing and taking care of a six-month-old boy; responsible for looking after the house and also for my commitments at work. I quit my work, moved back to India and re-located near my parents' house. My mother nursed and looked after my son whenever I wasn't around.'

'I am glad that you are not a bitter person as a result of all that has happened.'

'I looked at it this way—whatever is destined to happen, happens. Hence, why not accept the reality? It took me some time but I finally accepted it and forgave my wife. Ever since, I have found a friend in my son. We bond very well and he is my purpose to live. I have not looked for any other companion all these years and when Arun insisted that I get registered on the App, I reluctantly agreed. But, look, I found you.'

I blushed with embarrassment. I wanted to change the topic but he continued.

'There is something about you that compels me to believe that life should be given a second chance. Everything about you is subtle and calming. It attracts me and I have felt comfort in your company. After many years, I feel I want to share my life with someone and that someone seems to be you. I would love to know you more than just as a *friend.* I want to do my best and do justice to this relationship even though we are in different cities. Don't know what the future holds as raising my son carefully is a priority for me. Another marriage right away is out of question but the present seems to be just too beautiful and I would like to work towards making things happen eventually. It is important for me to know what you think and do you have any questions for me?'

He spoke for long, and I enjoyed being in the reverie that is a listener's prerogative. When he repeated, 'So, what do you think?' I awoke from the trance. I kind of liked him but was unprepared for such huge revelations. What Raghav had said was immense, but I knew I had to be honest with him.

'Well, this is a bit much for me to take but thank you for sharing. Sorry to hear about your marriage but your survival and comeback thereafter is commendable. I hope you and your son remain good pals to each other. Coming back to us—yes, I like you as a friend. There is a kind of a *connect* that seems to be brewing amongst us. I can see in you someone I would like to share my life with. However, at this point, neither am I ready to get into a commitment straightaway and nor do you seem to be all geared up for it. Just as you need to think about your son, so also, I need to think about *you, with your son*. I do not intend to *just take chances* anymore, after all that we both have gone through. Of course, your smoking does bother me but it will not much impact my decision. I know you for over three months now. I think you mean it when you say you will quit it.'

He looked at me and smiled before he called for the cheque. There was no need for any further words. I booked a cab for myself and while we both were waiting for it, Raghav said, 'This was one of the most splendid evenings of my life in a long time. I am here until 6 pm tomorrow. What about another cup of coffee? But only if you wish to....'

The cab meanwhile arrived. I smiled at him; we shook hands and bade goodbyes.

I pretended to not notice that his eyes looked sad. I sat in the cab and on the way, wiped my own moist eyes. There was certainly something bothering me somewhere. *Did I say the right things? Am I going to be serious about this relationship? Ought I to be? He has a son! An eight-year-old son! How will he and I accept each other? Am I getting into something very complicated? Should I just message him and tell him that nothing further is possible?* The questions did not stop plaguing my mind, till I reached home.

The next day, I could not concentrate much on anything else. I decided to go home early in the hope that my mind would become tranquil by the afternoon. It had been very restless, with thoughts tossing between my own confusion and his helplessness to commit fully to anyone. Yet, I could not completely stop thinking about him, for he was sensitive, charming and even wise. At the same time, there were many *what ifs… What if his son does not like me? What if he can't make up his mind even in the next five years? What if he is lying and simply wants to have a good time?*

At around 5 pm, I checked my cell, anticipating messages from Raghav but there were none. I decided to call him.

'Hello Raghav, am I disturbing you?'

'No, not at all,' he promptly replied. 'I just completed all my work and am heading back to the hotel to collect my luggage. Although, my flight is at 10 pm, I intend to check out all the coffee shops inside the terminal today.' He laughed saying this.

Words simply flew out of my mouth, 'Would you like to meet?'

His response was quick, 'Certainly, yes.'

'I know about a café which is on the way to the airport. It is not too far for me either. Shall send you the location, and see you in an hour.'

As we sipped our cappuccinos, I couldn't help but notice that Raghav kept looking at me every now and then. His eyes were seeking several answers but he remained tight-lipped.

Finally, I began, 'So, how was this visit to Delhi? Any different?'

'Aha! I would say it was extremely special this time,' said Raghav, winking mischievously.

Without beating around the bush, I asked, 'What if you cannot make up your mind for several years? What if your son does not agree?'

He was a bit startled, but quickly regained his composure and said, 'I do not know but I am sincere about trying to make things work out for us. As of now, I am letting time take its course but the opportunity to know someone as wonderful as you, is not worth letting go. Let us live in the moment! Don't you agree?'

I gulped the last sip of coffee, put down the mug and looked at him straight, 'You have been on my mind since last evening. I am not happy about what I said last night. I like you too, Raghav but I am a bit concerned.'

There was softness in his voice when he said, 'I understand your fears. I will do my best to make them recede gradually.'

We both looked at each other endearingly and smiled. It was time for Raghav to leave. We both walked towards our respective cabs. The hug that followed was spontaneous and full of warmth and hope.

As I sat in the cab, I sheepishly asked myself, *Did I just start dating?*

It was not springtime but there was spring in my steps and in my entire being. The breeze felt friendly as it caressed my cheeks and the air was fragrant and the skies were smiling graciously… I felt young. Over the next month or so, everyone around me kept commenting: Hey Leena, what's the matter? Is it love? Your face is glowing… Your eyes are brighter! Did you meet your 'someone special'?

The video calls in the weekends, the evening chats on weekdays and regular messages to share anything of consequence—were becoming the order of the day for me. Mom was observant and chose not to prod me for details. The receivers that every mother is blessed with, may be invisible to the world at large, but they are nevertheless the powerful-est ever and beyond the scope of an average human's comprehension! The antennas receive all signs and signals to near total accuracy and nothing ever escapes them.

One afternoon, as we both were lazing on the bed, she exclaimed, 'Isn't he a *Madrasi*?'

I was stunned. *How on earth did she know?* Before I could gather myself and recover from the jolt, she said in an amused tone, 'I know he is a Bengalurean *Madrasi* or some kind from the South. Hope you remember your earlier encounter with a *Tam-Bram*. It was a bitter-sweet experience, if you recall... And, Binnie, don't you think this one is also too dark? I had just peeped in once when you were on a video chat. I swear I did not listen to your conversation.'

'But Mom...,' I protested.

'*Beta*, I just casually remarked. I just want that you find someone who has a heart as nice as yours is. He should know your worth and that how precious you are. He should know how lucky he is to have you. I do not know if this one is going to be that guy, but I shall keep praying till you find one. A lot of stumbling blocks have come your way. You have been disappointed quite many times. You must be tempted by now to give it all up. But, don't do that. Whether this guy too—steps in or breaks your heart, I know not but you must not lose hope. There is a guy somewhere… and someday we shall find him. I know it.'

I struggled to find my voice even as she patted me on the arm and quietly slipped out of the room, saying, 'Binnie, I will make chai… Let us try the *besan laddoos* I made this morning.'

Haven't I already stuffed my system with enough laddoos? I wanted to say but then decided against arousing her ire or else, Mom for sure would throw the *besan laddoos* at me and my mouth could very well miss the aim.

She did not ask much in the days that followed, but her glances were quizzical. At the same time, she did not stop scanning more profiles for me and kept forwarding a few for my perusal.

It was after a month or so that one day when Raghav called, I said, 'Hey, why don't you fly down this weekend. I feel like meeting.'

His tone was a little defensive when he replied quickly enough, 'That is not possible, Leena. Weekends are exclusively for Suraj. Let me see if I can plan some work-related meetings in Delhi later this month.'

Though I sounded normal and told him very amiably, 'Oh, it is okay,' I felt a little strange. *Were we going to meet if and when his work came up in Delhi,* I wondered. The next moment, I chided myself, *of course, he has to work... He has to take care of his child. I cannot make such fanciful demands. Silly me!*

Over the next couple of months, Raghav and I met twice but our meetings (over a cup of coffee) were squeezed between finishing work and catching the return flight. I was, nevertheless, happy as Raghav was making an effort to catch up with me amidst everything else. A week after our last meeting, Raghav called one day. He was sounding unusually dull.

'Hey, is everything alright? What is wrong? Are you unwell? Hope you are not up to your usual pranks and fooling me....'

'My company has been on a downward spree for long. You know how start-ups are. Everything was happening right and then a glitch here and a loss there and then the slide commenced... I did try to make it spring back on its feet again but things are looking complex,' Raghav said, glumly.

'Oh, then? What next?'

'Talks are going on with a few buyers. I am pitching the ideas to a few investors in the coming months. I hope my employees can retain their jobs.'

'Oh, that is sad, indeed. Don't you worry, though. Life often takes unpredictable upward turns too. Is there something I can do?'

'No one can do anything, Leena. We will just have to wait and watch.'

Though I was concerned for him about this unexpected turn, I could not help but think about our fate. *Now what?* Another two months flew by. Raghav always sounded worried and dull whenever we spoke and he had already reduced the frequency of video calls.

At the breakfast table on a Sunday morning, Mom finally broke her silence, 'Leena, what is going on with you for over six months now? I see a change in you. Sometimes, you are very happy and on other days, you look dismal. Is it because of that *Madrasi* guy? Tell us clearly what it is… I have been sending you a lot of profiles but neither do you care to acknowledge nor reply. Is there something we should know about?'

A look of concern had spread its shadow on Papa's face too. He usually kept quiet and looked amused during such *I-dare-you* conversations initiated by Mom, but that day, he was visibly concerned.

'I am sorry... It's just that I was busy. And, no, there's nothing else. I will see them today,' was all I replied. I hurriedly completed my breakfast and went back to my room. Papa's worried face had left me disturbed. *Enough now,* I thought. *I need to know where we are headed. I understand what he is going through but I have my life too! What should I tell my parents? I am fine with waiting but until when?* With all these thoughts, I dialled Raghav. Though Sunday morning was strictly for Suraj, I decided to ignore the rule.

The phone kept ringing but no one answered.

I called once again in the afternoon. No answer.

I left a WhatsApp message at night.

Raghav called the next day. 'Hey, I am so sorry. I missed your calls yesterday. I was farming with Suraj at a farmhouse in the outskirts of the city. We planted a few seeds and plucked and washed some vegetables and then all of us, including my parents—we went to see another plot of land which my brother is considering buying.'

'Oh, but what if there was an emergency, Raghav? You could have at least taken the call or messaged. It would have hardly disturbed your happy family-time for two minutes,' I said, annoyed.

'I told you that I was with my kiddo and the rest of the family. I was just too busy.'

I did not like his reply but chose to avoid any further argument. 'Okay, I wanted to tell you that I have a lecture scheduled in S.M. College, Bengaluru next week. I was thinking that it will be a good opportunity to meet you and the kiddo over dinner.'

There was a pause at the other end and I could sense the tension. I gently asked, 'Hey, what happened? Aren't you happy to hear what I just said? We haven't met in months now, and I think it will be cool to meet Suraj, as well. I have heard such marvellous things about your kiddo that I can't wait to meet him.'

'What is the need to meet him, Leena? What will I tell him?' He sounded tired.

'Tell him we are friends. That is it. Doesn't it ever happen that you meet your friends with him over a casual dinner?'

There was another pause that lasted for a full one minute.

'No, I don't think this is a good idea,' replied Raghav, rudely.

'Why not?' This time I did not wish to avoid the discussion, which I knew was going to take an unpleasant turn.

'Because I don't think it is! Suraj has never seen me with any of my female friends.'

'I will come only the next week. Why don't you tell him that a friend is visiting from Delhi? Simple!'

'I said NO.' His voice was stern.

I tried replying in a calm voice, 'Raghav, what is the matter? Why this hesitation? We are not telling the kiddo that we are dating. Who in this world does not have friends and which kid will not understand that you have friends with whom you and he can dine?'

'Why are you not letting it go? I know my child… He will be upset. He has never seen me with another female. And, why this impatience? What has happened over the weekend? I did not know you were so stubborn!'

'What about me? You find me stubborn and impatient today but happily overlook the patience I have had all this while! I have been taking your dilly-dally attitude for quite some time now. I know things are rough at work but I don't find you capable of compartmentalising two different segments. Life goes on… The work-related ups and downs are there in everyone's life. If everyone waited for stability to set in permanently in one's profession, no one would marry until one's late fifties. Don't you think relationships are more important in life? I am not asking you to marry me tomorrow but let us at least discuss once in a while as to where are we going. There is no harm in taking a few strides at the personal front, despite the struggle at the professional one. I am just saying that let us, at least, meet—the three of us.'

Another pause ensued.

'Leena, I have too much on my mind. Right now, I cannot think of anything else other than my work. That's all!'

'Yeah, that is why you were farming the whole day yesterday! When everything else is going on as usual, and you can enjoy one full day with family—then why are we to put a halt at our front, for reasons unknown to me?'

'Look, I do not want to get into this unreasonable debate. I am too preoccupied right now. I don't think meeting the kiddo is a good idea at all. In fact, I think even we meeting at this time, is not a good idea. You come, give your lecture and make plans with other friends. I need time. Let me get over this state, and then I will come and meet you.'

'What do you mean—we meeting at this time is not a good idea?'

'Leena, I think I will call it quits for now. I cannot commit to anyone at this stage. Raising the kiddo is my priority and I realise that we may not head anywhere for the next 3–5 years. I don't want to hold you back.'

My worst fears were coming true. I remained in a dazed state for a moment or two, and then quickly regained composure. 'Is this your decision? Or, is it something on which you are contemplating? Do you want to sacrifice *us* for something like struggles-at-work or for a strange reservation that Suraj will not be able to take it? Tomorrow, your business might very well prosper but the hurt you are causing or the vacuum you are creating in mine and in your own life may not be filled.'

'Look here, Leena. If you are fine with our present arrangement, then it is alright with me too but, if you are looking for more—then, I think it is better to part ways. If things get better, I will come and see you.'

The matter-of-fact way in which he spoke—devoid of any emotion or hesitation, hurt me more than the actual words. The probability of me having erred again in recognising people, was staring at my face in full force. I wondered how and why did I find this guy mature and sensitive and how did I conclude that he could be that 'someone'? I was unafraid of putting the final nail in the coffin. I did not want to quit, with any *ifs* and *buts*.

'You will come to meet me when things get better, but what if your business goes down again after you come to meet me? Will you put *us* at stake again in a similar manner, as you are doing now?' I asked him in a flat voice.

'I don't know, Leena, what will happen and when. I am not an astrologer.'

'But, I know. I think I agree with your decision of calling it quits. I would rather be with me than be with someone who cannot distinguish and balance between unrelated events of his life. Thank you for all the good times, Raghav.'

'Leena, we can stay in touch,' Raghav pacified.

'Take care, do well,' I said and disconnected the call.

It was after a month and a half that I received Raghav's message saying, 'Hey, how are you, Leena? I am good. Things are now smooth and looking up at the work front. The company was taken over by an investor and I now head the IT division of it. Coming to Delhi next week, would you like to meet?'

'That is great, Raghav. Told you, things will change for good. All the best! I am a bit busy. I think I will skip.'

Fifteen days later, Mom and I were returning from a live concert of Arijit Singh, when I bumped into Arun in the parking lot. He was with a few of his friends and delighted to see me.

'Hi Leena, what a splendid surprise! Though I must say that I am a bit upset with you.'

'Why is that?' I asked with a look of surprise.

'Well, you just de-registered and quit from the App and did not give me any input or feedback either. How was your user-experience? You should not have been impatient. There are scores of people who have responded positively and said that they have found their soul-mates on it.'

Thank God! Mom is already seated in the car—I felt a wave of relief. However, I did not want to go on, on the said subject. To close the matter, I smiled and said, 'It is okay, Arun. I tried but I was not comfortable. Perhaps, not suitable for my types... Good luck to you, though!'

I was clutching the handle of the door of my car and my hand froze there after what I heard next.

'Leena, you should have earnestly tried. A far-flung cousin of mine—Rita, who is also single and is in her late thirties, met a good-looking, mature and a very charming guy from Bengaluru and they have started dating. And (laughing aloud) do you know the best part? The guy turned out to be my good pal, Raghav. See, this is how destinies unravel... No one knows what lies ahead, but we must try.'

It was dark, and mercifully, Arun may not have seen my face turn pale with disbelief. I managed to stutter: 'Wow...that is incredible! So, is your cousin getting married soon?'

'No *yaar*, it might take a while—is what Rita told me. Raghav has an eight-year-old son. He is not too sure of whether the young kid will be able to accept him with another woman. So, they have decided to take it slow and see how it all unfolds gradually….'

For the first time, Mom pressed the horn impatiently at the right moment! Arun could not see my wry smile as I said bye, and opened the door.

The Unkool Rendezvous

Why are people so muddled in their heads? How can they forever be clueless about where do they wish to go; what do they want to do? How can anyone be so confused so as not to know whether they wish to marry or not, and if they do wish to—whom do they want to marry and when?

Several such silly questions were popping in my head. But, I was not angry or even upset with Raghav. By the next morning, I was chuckling in amusement.

One look at Mom's face and I feared another stormy session not too far beyond. It was no big deal to infer that many questions must be jostling for space in Mom's mind and weighing her down. The only solace was that Mom allowed the questions a safe passage outside of her and onto my ears. At least I did not have to worry about hypertension building up pressure inside her, without a safe vent. I never had to wait for too long for the impending release.

'Binnie, why are you not clear about your own life? How can you be clueless about where do you wish to go, what do you want to do? How can anyone be so confused so as not to know whether one wants to marry or not? If you do wish to, whom do you want to marry and when?'

Errr, don't they sound a little familiar? How is Mom able to spy even on my thoughts—I asked myself as the barrage of questions fell on my ears with a thud.

Over the next few days, a few blockbuster-types were also aimed at me: 'Why do you think I have renewed the subscription of *shaadi-ka-laddoo.com?* Why are you simply rejecting the profiles left, right, and centre—since the past three-four months? What other options do you have? Tell me... Are you going to find someone on your own? I doubt if a miracle to that effect is written in my fate!'

I kept quiet, bearing her wrath.

One day, I took up the cudgels and dared to retort, 'I am exhausted and fed up. I do not feel like going through the same *hello-hi* drill on the online portal. The barrage of questions is too familiar and meaningless. *What do you do? Where do you work? Do you know how to cook? What do you think about starting a family? Why do you wish to remarry?* It is utter nonsense....'

During such episodes, Papa often popped up from his hiding place and offered a kind olive branch to the two highly strung bees. He did not fail in his duty this time either.

'Binnie, you are a wise girl. You handle your students in such a matured fashion. You have the knack to deal with all kinds of people in varying ways. In the same way, think and look at the proposals objectively and then decide how to respond to each one. Make efforts to connect with people, my dear girl.'

As soon as the domestic truce was thus established, Mom didn't miss her chance, 'I have just forwarded a profile to you. He is a Financial Consultant from Philadelphia, lives with his mother, and no issues from the previous marriage. Take a look, will you?'

I knew Mom was going to be persistent but I needed to pacify myself, at first. I had to have a talk with *me*. I went to the backyard of our house and perched myself on the hammock which remained tied in a quiet corner, over my favourite green patch where the grass grew wild and danced gleefully at the behest of the breeze. *I know… It is awkward. It is not easy either. Raghav was a nice guy and it is going to be hard to get over the whole thing but this remorse and regret has got to end… I have to be rational and yes, was I not sincere and did I not earnestly try to understand him, and even support him? I guess, my decision to move on is the best for both of us. The episode has concluded in a dignified way. Had I not put an end to it, it could have eventually gotten messy and painful for me and probably for him too.*

My conversation with myself lasted for about an hour, as there were too many intermittent visual breaks, when the memories of moments spent with him flooded my mind. It took some stern cajoling before the mind agreed to castaway the visuals in some remote corner and agreed to eventually delete them. However, I also chided my mind for promising me the skies… *Who has ever been able to delete the memories? Who has ever succeeded in the impossible?*

Tempted though I was to call Chirag for I knew that he was probably the only one who would not get animated or passionate about the whole thing and most importantly, he would never judge me, I nevertheless hesitated this time. I clutched my cell phone hard but did not call. *Why is this happening? Why am I not calling him? Why am I thinking so much? Will he soon be exasperated by my relentless ranting about not finding the 'right' guy?* I pushed all my doubts aside and called him.

'Hey, how are you? What's happening?'

'Hey Leena, lovely to hear from you. I thought you were going to go to the theatre for a play.'

'No, did not feel like going. I am just swinging idly on the hammock and mulling over what has happened.'

'Why? What has happened? How is Raghav? All is well between you two? Please do not tell me that he too has disappointed you….'

I hesitated momentarily, but then came out with it all. There was silence at the other end, though I had finished.

'Chirag, are you there?'

'Yes, I am here, Leena. Honestly, I do not know what to say. In fact, you may not even like it if I did say what I am feeling right now.'

'No, I won't. Say it all… I am listening.'

'Leena, you cannot deny that I have so far always been very unbiased and non-judgmental at least as far as you and your affairs are concerned. I do not know why but I have always empathised with you…wished only the good for you. I have sincerely hoped that you find just the kind of guy as would complement you; be compatible with you….'

There was a long pause.

'I am listening, Chirag. You need not hold back.'

'Hmm… I know I need not hold back but I am really worried about your reaction. If I tell you to seriously wonder as to why do you keep coming across all these weirdos, you might be offended. Seriously, Leena, have you spent one moment thinking about it? Why? Why is there not a single normal guy, and a natural conclusion to the interludes? Perhaps, it is because although you are looking for a perfect package deal, you are yourself not exactly clear about what is it that you are ready to offer from your end. And seriously, have you let go of all your fears, insecurities, doubts and apprehensions about men?'

'But...' I stopped myself in time. My heart was beating wildly. *I thought he is a true friend...and all this while, this is how and what he thought of me?*

'Please, let me complete, Leena. On several occasions, I felt like showing you the mirror but then thought that since you are otherwise such a level-headed girl, you would eventually introspect and see the picture clearly. Of course, I do not deny that most of these guys have been nuts. Sadly, you have had to put up with the freaky outcomes of their eccentricities. I am not worried about them but I am worried about what all these encounters are likely to and are doing to you. Can't you see, Leena? Every such episode chips off one corner in you and adds to the cynicism; makes you further wary, suspicious and bitter. Be it Sanjay or Saurabh or now Raghav, either you could not see clearly what they had to offer you or you were too obsessed about finding in them what your eyes wanted to see. Or perhaps, you were one moment in it and the next minute, as if you were waiting for it all to crumble and when it did, your fears stood vindicated and somewhere you heaved a sigh of relief. Tell me honestly, who were you seriously willing to give your one hundred percent to? Without misgivings and reluctance?

And sometimes, you plunged headlong without so much as a thought and at other times, you started off with doubts and unwillingness to commit. Am I wrong?'

I did not know what to say. I was stupefied by his words. *Was he accusing me of expecting too much or of being self-centred? Or, as he said: was I being too hasty in my estimates and initiatives? No, I think he just has a poor opinion of me and that is why his judgments are coloured… And, I had shared with him everything, without as much as an iota of care.*

'Leena, I am waiting for an answer.'

'Ahem, oh, yeah… Yes! You are right. I need to think a lot. I… I need to think… Shall we speak later, if you don't mind?'

'No, Leena! Wait! Do not disconnect just like that. Are you hurt? I need to know this much… I….'

I interrupted him. 'Chirag, please… Not now! Later, please… Bye.'

I got up from the hammock, washed my face, and returned to my room with a steaming cup of *adrak* chai for myself. I sat down and closed my eyes. I could hear Chirag's words clearly and distinctly. *Was he telling me the truth? Is it my fault that I am attracting either the wrong kind of guys or my subsequent actions are wrong after the initial exchanges? What is it that I needed to do? How do I change all of it myself? How do I erase all my fears and confusions? If I have misgivings, what do I do?*

I was surprised at myself that I did not break down or cry at the way Chirag had laid bare my flaws. His words had stunned me but did not unnerve me. I knew there was no magic wand I had which I could wave and erase all my negativity. *Why not let life take its own course,* I asked myself wryly. *I will go on till I am ready to call it quits and face Mom head-on... If my fears are to be erased, they shall be erased when I meet someone I am meant to spend the rest of my life with.*

I was not altogether convinced with my logic but decided it was enough and my head could take it no longer. *Let me try and sleep and I shall feel better in the morning,* I assuaged myself.

In the fortnight that followed, Chirag and I did not exchange messages or call each other. The silence, it was apparent, was working well for both of us. Of course, I was tempted many times during each day to call but I did not. It was important to not come across as weak-kneed. Exams, assignments and field trips kept me busy in college and I returned home exhausted and late all through the fortnight.

Mom must have, expectedly, sensed that something was amiss and had wisely decided to not rummage through. One evening, I returned home late in the afternoon and sat staring at my laptop, contemplating whether to open my mailbox. Eventually, I did. Mom's message was beckoning me from the top. I clicked it to open.

'I am a 38-year-old Financial Consultant and an American citizen. I was married briefly for six months, thereafter we separated due to lack of compatibility. Details can be discussed. I live with my mother. I like trekking and I also practise meditation. I liked your profile. May we connect?'

The guy meditates! I clicked on the 'Accept' box and moved on to complete a few assignments I had brought home from college.

Two days passed and I had almost forgotten about it when I received a forwarded message from Mom: 'Thanks for accepting my invite, Leena. Would you like to connect? My email is manik_kapoor@gmail.com. Drop a line please, anytime.'

At about **1 pm**, the next day, I wrote to him:

Hello Manik,

Got your message. Sending a text mail to connect. We can chat sometime.

Thanks

Leena.

At 7 pm

Hi Leena,

Happy to connect… How is it going for you? I am actually travelling for work, and will return over the weekend. You know how a consultant's job is… Always keeps one on the toes. I sometimes feel like quitting but then I remind myself of the bills. ☺ Tell me about yourself.

Take care,

Manik.

Next day, 10 pm

Yes, I know… To become a consultant is a much-coveted desire of many but one almost pays through the nose for such a profile :) I am sure that it remunerates enough to cover your bills though :) I am a lecturer at a college in Delhi. Year after year, I teach the same concepts and facts… Only the faces which listen to me keep changing, but I am not complaining. I like what I do.

Leena.

@3 am

What a fulfilling job you have! Empowering students with knowledge, year after year. We only work for ourselves, whereas you work for others. I am impressed. What are your other interests?

Manik.

@7 am

Good morning, Leena,

Today is the last day on this special assignment, before I return home. Would you like to chat on Sunday? Please note my number: +01....

@4 pm

Hi Manik,

Safe trip home. Yes, Sunday 9 pm suits me, if that works for you. My number is +91....

@11 pm

Yes, Sunday 9 pm IST works for me fine!

Manik.

It was only at 9.15 pm on Sunday that it struck me that I was to chat with Manik at 9 pm. Hurriedly, I picked up my cell. There was a WhatsApp message from Manik:

'Hello Leena, I am here online, ten minutes earlier than the scheduled time—knowing that you are a teacher and that they are always on time. I thought I better not give you any reason to punish me. Ha! Ha! Hello? Are you there?'

Another message @9.10 pm

Manik: 'Hey, I am still here. Will hang around for some time ☺'

@9.20 pm

Me: 'Hi, am so sorry, Manik. It completely slipped out of my mind.'

Manik: 'Hey, Leena. It is fine. It happens.'

Me: 'No, no… I am so sorry. It usually does not happen.'

Manik: 'So, what was special about today? What made you forget our online rendezvous, if I may ask? ☺'

Me: 'Oh no, nothing special. I was watching a movie and I just got immersed into it until five minutes ago when I recollected all of a sudden that we were to chat on WhatsApp ☺'

Manik: 'Which movie?'

Me: '*Kabhi Alvida Na Kehna.*'

Manik: 'Wow, that's a deep choice. I like that movie.'

Me: 'Yeah, it is one movie which can be counted as one amongst the best ones of Abhishek Bachchan. Anyway, how was your trip on the whole?'

Manik: 'Oh, it was work, as usual. However, this time I did make an effort to see a bit of Florida after the work hours. I never explore places; for me, it has always been just work and nothing more. Don't know if it is because there is nobody along to enjoy with or is it merely an excuse for I am too exhausted after work to embark on a sight-seeing plan. Do you like to travel, Leena?'

Me (typed with full gusto): 'Oh, yesssssss! I love to travel. Have been to a few places with family, and have taken some solo trips and on a few occasions, have travelled due to work.'

Manik: 'SOLO travel! That is totally cool. The experiences too must have been one of a kind. . . .'

The next one hour simply whizzed past in knowing each other's interests and almost the same routine drill that I had gone through in the last year and a half.

Yeah, it all starts the same way, I reminded myself! *I have to be patient*—I remembered Papa gently exhorting me to be so.

With a firm resolve to not be judgmental at the very outset, I concluded the chat with a mutually expressed hope to connect again.

I slept fitfully that night.

I was unusually busy over the next two days. It was only on the following Wednesday night that I checked my personal mails. There was a mail from Chirag. With a pounding heart, I opened the mail:

> Hello there, hope you are quite calm and composed by now. What is this, Leena? Should we sulk as teenagers? ☺ Come on, be a sport and let us resume our chats and long talks. I am missing them, dearie... I apologise for being so blunt and that too, all of a sudden. No doubt, you must have been speechless for some time. I am sorry, not for saying what I did but for saying it all at once and abruptly.
>
> Game for a no-holds-barred debate on Trump's latest salvo at immigrants? You tell the time....

I grinned broadly. It seemed all was going to be fine once again. I began humming my favourite song and continued checking my mailbox.

There were three mails from Manik.

Monday @5 am

> Hey Leena,
>
> It was great chatting with you. You come across as a sensible, intelligent and a witty woman. I like that you do not rely on others when it comes to exploring new things—unlike me, who sits and makes excuses. It will be nice to chat again.
>
> Take care,
>
> Manik.

Monday @7 am

Hey, have a good week ahead!

Wednesday @4 am

How is it going? You seem to have vanished! I am inspired by you and have decided to drive down two hours from my place to a water park this Saturday—all by myself! Hurray! Finally! Not sure how good will my company be but let's see... When I return, I shall tell you all ☺ Are you available to chat same time on Sunday?

Manik.

Wednesday @8 pm

Hey Manik.

How are you? I am fine. Good to know about your weekend plan to venture and enjoy all by yourself. Yes, Sunday looks good.

Enjoy your trip!

Best,

Leena.

Sunday @9 pm on WhatsApp

Me: 'Hey, this time, I'm on time ☺'

Manik: 'Well...well... Not bad! How are you doing, Leena? Hope your week was a nice one.

Shall I call you if you don't mind? I hate to type such a lot.'

Me: 'Well, yes… I guess talking will be easier.'

Manik called me. He sounded like he was one worn-out guy; someone who lives a dreary life. The tone was flat and drab. 'Hi, finally we speak! So, how was your week?'

'Hello, Manik… Yes, it started well, and then poof! It was gone! You tell me about your solo trip experience. I am eager to know how it was.'

'Well, it was a bit uncomfortable at first but then I gradually adjusted with myself. In fact, the silence all along the way…sitting on a ride all alone and then sharing the thrill and joy with oneself at the end of it—was not easy but I think it was good that I tried. I may just keep getting better at it. Thank you, Leena. You have already brought me a little closer to myself.'

We both shared a laugh, and then there was a brief pause.

Manik then said, 'Leena, is it alright if we talk a bit now about the purpose for which we are in touch? Are you fine with that?'

Ah, we have come to it finally… I sighed but not softly.

'Yes, please… Tell me.'

Manik began, 'As I had mentioned earlier, I was married and we separated after six months of marriage. I took my time to move on and now feel ready to start afresh in life. I live with my mother. When my wife came to the US after our wedding, she was fine initially but within two months, she started complaining about my mother living with us and insisted on her moving out. I tried to dissuade her but it did not help much. She wanted us to live in some other house. Finally, after three months of marriage, we moved into a new place which was not far from my mother's house. I was not happy but gave in, thinking that it will keep peace. But, after a month, she started fighting about why I visited my mother twice a day, and that I should cut down on the money I give to my mother to run her house and so on. It was unacceptable to me that despite moving away from my mother, she was not happy. We started fighting over silly matters and the daily arguments led to ugly fights. One day, she asked me for a divorce. I did not make any effort to reconcile and we separated. She moved back to India and I moved back with my mother.'

Is he a Mama's boy? His revelations made me wonder. 'I am sorry to hear that, Manik.'

'What about you? What went wrong in your marriage?' Manik questioned.

'Well Manik, I am not comfortable sharing it all so soon. For now, I can say that there were compatibility issues and we mutually separated. Let's get to know a little more about each other, first. Is it okay?'

He replied gently, and in a calm tone. 'That is fine. May I share a little more with you?'

I suppressed a groan. 'I am listening.'

'Ever since I have moved in with my mother, I feel *pulled back* all the time. I feel as if I exist only to meet the demands of the house or to do Mom's chores. My friends have distanced themselves from me as I have not been giving them any time. I am always by my mother's side, trying my best to meet her expectations. I think I am losing my confidence. Often, I feel unable to express myself. I dither, even while engaging in a simple conversation with others. As a result, I feel pent up within myself. I need a friend, a partner to help me come out of this state. And after talking with you, I think you can help me. Will you help me to find myself, Leena?'

I felt uneasy in the gut. *It seems to be another case of someone needing not an entire person but rather, a shoulder of just about anybody.* I felt miserable. I looked up (though did not dramatically raise my hands in the air in Mom's style) and cast a piteous look at whoever was up there. *Why no normal guy for me? Where are all those wholesome and fitful guys who do not need mothers, babysitters, counsellors and motivators? Am I never going to find one?* I didn't realise when I uttered a loud sigh and exclaimed, 'Who? Me?'

The next instant, I regretted my rude response. 'Oh, I'm sorry. Okay, sure… But, errr… I… How can I be of any help? I don't know your situation completely. I suggest that you engage yourself in activities which reinforce mindfulness. I had read in your profile that you meditate. Why don't you then join a yoga class, or connect with groups that harness our potential at thinking independently, speaking in public and expressing oneself creatively? You can perhaps start the process by first having a clear talk with your mother. You must explain to her patiently that you do have a life of your own and you too need to be involved with other people and in other activities.'

In a very weary tone, he said, 'Hmm… I do need to. In fact, I know and I also decide to do this and that… But, all of a sudden there is either an onslaught of some chores spelt out by Mom or I just don't feel up to it and I retreat.'

'Your sense of resolve seems to have weakened over the years. Why don't you begin with a regular bout of exercising? Go for an occasional run, consistent brisk walks, or even swimming! You will start feeling good about yourself in no time. I have read somewhere that when we exercise or laugh, endorphins are produced and released and they make us feel good. Go out with your friends and watch movies, or even go on a solo trip and make new friends.'

There was silence at the other end. *Phew! Was it too much?* 'You there, Manik?'

When he replied, there was a sudden fiery element in his tone, 'Brilliant! You are such an inspiring person, Leena. I knew it. I was right about you. You have a spark in you. You will go a long way. You will become famous one day. Why don't you upload your motivational talks or videos on *YouTube*? You will rock!'

I blushed, 'Oh no, please! Don't praise me this much. I just said what anyone would have ordinarily told you.'

Either I had spoken too much or I was just plain exhausted because I was suddenly aware that it was well past bed-time. I told him so, 'Manik, guess it is getting too late now. I get up early for college. Well, then... Bye from me!'

'Thank you, Leena. I am certainly going to do something about my life now... I feel all charged up! Can we connect more often so that I feel inspired, motivated and can also clear my doubts, if I have any?'

I was hesitant, and naturally so. I was not much keen to assume the responsibility of implanting pep talks on his dreary mind-set.

'You can drop me emails and yes, we can chat or talk on WhatsApp once in a while. And it is not important or necessary for you to try out everything that I said. Simply listen to your heart! And you will feel the difference,' I feebly offered.

'See, another inspiring thought! Thank you so much, Leena. I think I have found a true friend, confidante and guide,' he gushed.

I was unsure of my own feelings at that moment. *Perhaps, endorphins will be released in my body and I will feel good when I would have made a difference in someone's life,* I assured myself before setting foot in the world of dreams, or errr, nightmares?

Monday @2 am. Message on WhatsApp.

Hey Leena,

You are an angel. I am glad I met you. Everything that you said is so true. I need to help myself. Did I tell you that I am financially quite secure? I earn almost $8,000 every month, and my estimated savings are over $300,000. Yet I feel scared and nervous when I think about my future. I keep working harder and saving money but I don't feel satisfied. I want to meditate… I try but I am unable to. Will you give me a few tips on how to make the mind a little still; a little calm?

Can we talk tonight at 9 pm your time?

I read and re-read Manik's message. There was something which I felt was not right... Some strange and unpleasant thoughts seemed to be gnawing me. *Should I discuss it with Chirag?* I debated with myself. *After all, we were jolly old pals once again and spoke every other day on every other matter.* The dilemma lasted for full five minutes. I called Chirag and told him all about Manik. He was quiet for several moments. I began to get goosey. *Will he blast again*?

'Leena, do you really want to know what I think? Well, I think you are neither a counsellor, nor an agony aunt. You are asking me if you should be connecting further with this guy. Seriously, are you kidding me? Well, I think he seems to be so not in control of his life. Would a normal guy reveal his financial details to someone who he has just met online, and that too, being a financial consultant himself? Moreover, he is so indecisive and his life seems to be in a mess. You've got to stay away.'

I replied to Manik:

Manik, tonight is not possible. You may find meditation courses for beginners, online. Look up *YouTube*, and even download some relaxing music and try to follow your breath. Good luck.

You can drop me an email. We will talk another day.

Monday @8 pm

Leena,

Sorry, I am such a dud. I know the week has just started for you but I have to tell you that you can make many wandering souls like me see the path. I told my mother today that I will go out with friends for a movie on Sunday. Thank you so much, Leena. You changed my life!

Tuesday @2 pm

Good to know that, Manik. You will figure out your way soon.

Good luck!

Leena.

Tuesday @9 pm

Hey, I was just hoping that if you are free, will call you. Take care.

Wednesday @5 am

Good morning, Leena.

A reluctant me, same day @12.30 pm

Hey, have a good week ahead, Manik.

Thursday @4 am

Hello, Angel Leena!

I just looked up your social media profiles. I must say, there is something divine about your face. You look like a healer. I think, we have a connection from previous lives and you have come as a saviour in this life for me. What would I have done without you! Thank you so much, Leena.

Thursday @10 pm

Me: Hey Manik, can we talk 9 pm tomorrow?

This time round, I was sure that I had to talk to him.

The next day, Manik called at 9 pm. 'Hey Leena, how is everything with you?'

'Fine.' I had decided to keep it swift and short.

'You are such a divine....'

I interrupted him, 'Hey... Hey... Manik. Please, stop all that. I am living with an uncomfortable feeling since the past few days; in fact, ever since we connected. You wanted to share about your life and I sincerely tried to be empathetic. I gave you a few suggestions, and that's all. Please do not eulogise me. I did not know then, whether the suggestions would or would not help you but I tried doing my bit. Now, however, it is getting too stuffy for me. I would like to wrap up our short rendezvous. I sincerely wish you luck in changing your lifestyle and overcoming your fears but I feel my role therein was a short one and is over now.'

'Oh… Oh no! I am so sorry…so sorry. I don't know how it happened and when it happened but I regret that I made you feel uncomfortable. Please, I beg you, give me another chance. I will be careful in the future,' Manik said, apologetically.

An uncanny feeling of unease was almost stifling me now. 'No Manik, please excuse me. I wish you luck in all your efforts but I feel it is best to wrap up here. Got to go, and you take care. Goodbye.'

There was silence at the other end. I disconnected. I was sure that though I was brief I was not curt.

Saturday @1 am. Message on WhatsApp.

Hey, I am sorry, Leena.

Saturday @2 am

Can you give me another chance, please?

Saturday @4 am

Will you please talk with me tonight at 9?

Sunday @10 am

I think, you will not reply. Take care. Bye!

E-mail after a month…

Hey Leena,

Hope you are good. I am actually very happy and doing fantastic. Just wanted to let you know that after you turned me down, I met another girl from Delhi on *shaadi-ka-laddoo.com*. Unlike you, she is not rude and we talk every day. She is more beautiful than you are and is a doctor. By the way, did I tell you that you need to apply a little make-up and take some efforts on improving your persona? You come across as very dull from your profile pictures. And, only if you speak a little sweetly will you make some headway and find a groom.

I am coming to Delhi next month to meet my girlfriend and then we are going to Europe for two weeks. So bad! It could have been you but you see, your loss is someone else's gain. ☺

My advice to you: make up your mind soon about marrying someone, or else you will continue to wait for Mr Perfect and grow old. Already, you are not so young.

Anyway, I have to go now to shop for my girlfriend. All the best to you.

Manik

A Sugary-Syrupy Specimen

This time on, I could not have possibly called Chirag to tell how my story (the bitter comments that the tangy *laddoo* called Manik had written to me) concluded. Of course, the story this time round was not as full of sobs, as it was full of *sighs-of-relief* and yet I was not feeling entirely at-ease. I was aware, that of late, thoughts of Chirag were occupying a lot of space in my mind. *Am I being drawn towards him?* I mused often at the thought, and inevitably always brushed it under the carpet. *Come on, do not entertain such silly thoughts. Good friends are good as long as they remain friends. Who knows if he is married, committed or unengaged? And even if unattached now, who knows with whom he might like to spend his life? After all, there may be no dearth of options....*

The other day, while casually checking my Facebook account, I was drawn once more to Tara's profile. There were no updates after that last photo I had seen of Chirag and her in the group. I almost once thought of asking Chirag about her, on our next chat but then again, I recalled the spat we had when I had attempted prying into his personal life. For both of us, it had left a bitter taste.

I held my shoulders straight, looked up and reminded myself, *I am and I feel complete and open to sharing my completeness with someone who can be my significant other—not the better half!*

One thing that had notably altered in life in the past year and half was that I had begun to dread Sundays. Either Sundays were chosen by Mom to remind me to *come down on Earth* or they were filled with sagas and sob stories of the *laddoos* I had been chatting with. *Why are none of the laddoos sweet*? I uttered these last words and looked up at the Almighty, with a vexed expression. (The Angels seemed to have chosen that very moment to say…*Amen!* And, oh! How I regretted those words in the days that followed!)

Coming back to Sundays, *Alas! Where did those fun-and-mischief-filled Sundays disappear, when Shaurya and I planned adventures; did culinary experiments that maddened Mom and the house reverberated with laughter and popcorn strewn all over the floor as we watched movies back-to-back?* I pined for those days when life was not so full of care; and there was time to stand and stare.

And the dread-filled Sundays arrived far too soon and often. Mom summoned me into her room one Sunday. She wore a determined and grim expression on her face. Papa had that resigned look on his face, which meant that he had valiantly tried to fight a battle for me but had lost the war. I sat down on the couch and braced myself for what lay ahead.

'I have consulted a few trusted astrologers. There is a flaw in your horoscope and that is why we are reaching nowhere.'

'Excuse me!' I exclaimed. Nothing could have prepared for this startling discovery.

'No, *you* please excuse me! To rectify the imbalance in the position of your stars, you need to marry a *matka* in a ceremony in the temple.' She said so matter-of-factly, as if girls everywhere were marrying earthen pots and it was a routine affair.

'WHAT! Marry an earthen pot? You mean a *mitti ka matka*?' I almost screamed.

'Why? What is the matter? It is a simple remedy Sharma*ji*—your Papa's palmist friend has suggested. You ought to be thankful that there is a remedy.'

'NO! I am never going to be a party to such nonsense! Who do you think I am? An object, which is devoid of feelings and also devoid of rationality? Well, in case you forget, you have raised me as a rational adult. I can think and take my decisions. And, did you also forget that I teach in a college? Is this what I must be telling my students? That if you are unable to get married, go and marry an earthen pot at first and all the defects shall be taken care of?'

I was unstoppable but somewhere in the midst of my strong verbal outburst, I heard loud sobs.

I stopped. Mom was crying. It is one of the last and the finest instruments mothers universally use for the purpose of fishing out a resigned nod of affirmation from their wards. Her wailing intensified, and Papa's attempt at mollifying her, was brushed aside with a firm hand.

My heart melted and tone softened.

'Mom, please try and understand me. I cannot do all of this... It is just not being me.'

Mom, while still sniffing and tears flowing down her eyes: 'Binnie, you do not have to do a thing. I will handle it all. You have to just do a few tasks mechanically, at the behest of your mother who loves you so much. I want to see you happily settled. Do it for my sake; for our sake.'

At the last few words, she looked at Papa and extracted a nod in total unison. She continued, 'You have to just briefly marry an earthen pot and it will be offered to the Ganges. I have booked a room at a resort in Rishikesh, and arranged for a *Panditji.* We shall take a flight tomorrow afternoon, that is Wednesday, and Thursday is a holiday. You won't miss college and we shall be back on Thursday evening. I know I have taken the liberty to organise everything without asking you but *beta,* I am worried for you... Do you want me to fold hands and request you to please do this for me?'

I did not reply. The sobs became louder.

'Please, Binnie,' she mumbled in between her sobs.

I decided to go along and nodded gravely. She looked up as one looks up at the sky when the sun emerges out from behind the clouds on a grey day.

Wiping her tears with a corner of her dupatta, she tried to sound cheerful, 'Take it as a short getaway, dear. Didn't we both love Rishikesh the last time we visited together? And the resort is the finest in town.'

All this while, Papa had not said a word. I could see a trace of relief on his face too. *Was he an equal accomplice*?

I hope they have not printed the wedding cards: 'We solicit your benign presence on the pious occasion of our daughter Leena joining in matrimony with Mr…errr Mr Matka,' I murmured as I left their room.

As soon as Mom thought I was out of earshot, she told Papa, 'Don't you know Aishwarya Rai married a tree before marrying Abhishek? Look at them today… They are a perfect couple with a beautiful daughter.' Papa uttered a quiet *hmmm*….

I returned to face her and quip sarcastically, 'Oh, by the way, Mom—haven't you made a plan to go shopping at Ushnak Mal & Sons in South Ex for my D-day outfit?' She felt the sting. I could see fire in her eyes—fiercer than the high flame of the gas burner on which *rajma* had been simmering in the kitchen.

I was quiet the next day and the day after. We boarded the flight. Mom, though relieved that I had agreed, looked concerned.

Oh mothers! Their concern is matchless and unrivalled, I thought to myself. *Why make it all difficult for her? If I am doing this for her, I might as well do it with a smile.* I looked at her and squeezed her hand reassuringly. She smiled in return, even as her eyes looked moist.

The Shanti Aloha Resort at Rishikesh was splendid indeed! Nestled amidst the graceful forests and overlooking the divine Ganges—it cast a blissful effect on those who stepped in its precincts. Though I had been virtually dragged into it, I nevertheless felt happy at just being there, in the moment.

Our room was simple but aesthetically designed. After we settled in, we decided to go down to the restaurant for lunch. On our way, we bumped into a newlywed couple, who were apparently staying in the same resort. Mom, as expected, smiled at them and they returned the smile and a casual talk followed on the weather and the like. They were a gregarious pair, eager to dole out the bubbles of joy, popping in their hearts!

'We are from Mumbai, and have come to *Devbhoomi* for our honeymoon. We came here yesterday, from Mussoorie and en route to Ranikhet,' the jolly young guy gave the unsolicited info to Mom even as the petite bride blushed crimson.

The poor guy had no clue that he had touched a raw nerve somewhere, and was surprised to see Mom's facial expressions change suddenly. She congratulated them and with a 'Best wishes to both of you', she moved forward, beckoning me to follow.

The brief encounter changed Mom's mood. She nibbled at her food in a disinterested sort of way. Meanwhile, I took a second serving of *moong dal halwa,* despite Mom looking none too pleased with my foray.

'Binnie, be ready for tomorrow. We must reach the *mandir* by 8 am. The ceremony will be over in two hours and then we can do sightseeing or shopping before we fly back in the evening. Let us be here for the *Ganga aarti* this evening.'

'Suits me, Mom.'

We were dead tired by the end of the evening. Both of us simply crashed out and slept like logs.

In the middle of the night I felt as if something was moving. It seemed the bed or some other furniture was shaking. I opened my eyes and tried to make sense of it in the dark. There were soft voices coming from somewhere. It took me an instant to realise that the shaking and the noises were happening in the room next door, presumably occupied by the newlyweds. Everything seemed to be shaking in the room and then the whispers and moans reached the zenith and then completely stopped.

Oh, God! I whispered, for I did not have the guts to look in the direction of Mom and check if she was asleep or awake. *Please…oh, please—let her be asleep,* I hoped fervently. I knew though, that it was difficult for anyone to not be awakened by the loud noises. It was one of the most awkward moments of my life and I knew that it would be so for Mom too.

On Day Two, I felt a little funny and a lot apprehensive at what was about to happen. Sitting in the temple premises, I decided not to take it all too seriously. I tried looking at the funny side of it and giggled and resolved that if I ever write a book on my crusades to find my very own private groom, I will certainly write about this escapade. It must go down in my autobiography as a moment when I bravely endured the unthinkable. I was seated next to a beautifully adorned *matka* in front of the *havan kund*.

In a hushed tone, I whispered into Mom's ears: 'By the way, Mom, your son-in-law looks pretty dashing, having arrived straight-from-the-parlour today, for the wedding.'

Mom shot an angry glance at me.

The *Panditji* was blabbering chants which neither of us understood (by us I mean—Mom and I; not the *matka* and I).

The sense of discomfort reached its pinnacle when I was made to take seven rounds of the fire holding my beloved groom in my hands. It was unbelievably awkward.

Finally, the discomfiture eased and the *matka* was offered to the Ganges. The *Panditji* took his fee and fruits and Mom let out a sigh of relief, followed by a prophecy in a triumphant tone, 'You will be married soon now, Binnie.'

The flight back home was fun as both of us chattered incessantly and exchanged all the unstated gossip of the past few months. Meanwhile, on and off I chuckled umpteen times, recalling my *pheras* with the earthen pot (errr, my groom) and then drowning it (or him?) mercilessly.

A mischievous thought struck me and with a straight face, I asked Mom, 'Mom, should I edit my profile on *shaadi-ka-laddoo.com* and add "married twice"—once to a human, and the other time, to a *matka* and that am now looking for a human once again?'

'Keep quiet, Binnie!'

Two days later, I came home from an extended day at work to find Mom smiling. 'Now what?' I asked, guardedly.

'*Beta*, I spoke with Shailesh this morning. Oh, what a sweet boy he is.'

'Shailesh, who?'

'Oh ho, on *shaadi-ka-laddoo.com*—I was just scanning some profiles when Shailesh's profile came up. I liked his picture and then I read about him. By the way, Binnie, I downloaded the *shadi-ka-laddoo.com* app on my mobile today. Cool, *na*! I can now see the profiles at one click. Wait, let me read his vital stats,' Mom announced.

I waited for the usual raving of the guy's features but none came. Presumably, he did not have anything 'vital' to show off. *Must be an average-looking guy and hence Mom is so quiet,* I knew.

'His looks are okay; not great but that is fine. I found him nice. We want a good heart, dear, for beauty fades with time,' Mom said, pensively.

I did not interrupt her, and let her continue.

Apparently, she had more to say, 'I liked him and sent an Invite to connect. Then, when I saw he was online, I sent a message and he instantly responded. He said namaste to me and then praised your profile. He asked me if he could call and I gave him my number. Binnie, I cannot tell you how sweet he sounded when he spoke. He came across as the most chivalrous boy I have so far known. He enquired in general about me, your father's well-being and gave regards to all in the family. He was so polite that he very gently asked if he could connect with you on your personal number.'

I was about to open my mouth to make a fuss, when I heard Mom continuing, 'Where does one find such modest guys anymore? I am telling you that I am so very impressed with this one, I told him to call you tonight at 9.'

I made up my mind to protest, when Mom spoke yet again, '*Beta,* I have made your favourite *kadhi-chawal* today. Please, freshen up, have your food and speak with him.'

Mom is clearly in awe of this Shailesh. There is no point in arguing and as it is, I am not doing anything in the evening, I reasoned with myself.

@9 pm

Shailesh sent a message on WhatsApp: 'Namaste, is that Leena*ji*? I am Shailesh here. Spoke with your mother today morning and got your number. Can we chat?'

He is greeting me with 'Namaste' and 'ji'? What is wrong with him?

Me: 'Hey Shailesh… Yes, Mom did mention about you to me. How are you? Let us talk.'

Shailesh called and I answered, 'It will be nice to talk, isn't it?'

'Yes, Leena*ji*. How was your day?'

It was difficult for me to gather what he was saying. He was so very soft in his tone and speech. I actually had to press the phone closer to my ear in order to hear him.

I replied, 'It was fine. What about your day?'

In a more deferential tone than before, Sailesh replied, 'I woke up, made tea for myself and for Mom and then had a chat with my plants and am now speaking with you.'

Mom was right, I felt. To be honest, I had not come across a man in the recent times who was as genteel as this guy was. *And he talks to his plants*!

'Leena*ji,* may I begin by telling about myself?'

And, here it comes… I sat comfortably on the bed, with my legs crossed—ready for another roller-coaster ride!

'Yes, please.'

'Leena*ji,* I was born and raised in Canada. My parents moved here for work early in their lives. My father died when I was ten years old. Mom is a school teacher, and my sister is married and lives in Ontario. We stay in Brampton. We live together—my mother and I. I am an electrical engineer and am looking for someone who can be my friend. My first marriage did not work out due to incompatibility. I like to read during my leisure time and weekends are mostly stocking up the groceries or occasional visits to my sister's place. Do you like kids, Leena*ji*?'

Shailesh was talking in a glazed tone...and with too many pauses in between, as if a bag of saccharine was tied with his vocal chords, and whenever he spoke, the contents of the saccharine bag fell and were mixed with the sound that came out of him. And, in the entire process—he paused in between. *At this rate, I will become a diabetic soon,* I suppressed a giggle. The pauses in his talk were longer than the sentences he spoke.

'Yes, I do like kids.' I decided not to dwell much on the subject further.

'Leena*ji*, may I ask what happened in your case? What problems came up in your first marriage?'

'Well, we too had compatibility issues. Eventually, we fell out after five years of staying in a relationship that had turned pretty sour.'

He murmured some words (I could not decipher) in a sympathetic tone.

'I can understand your pain, Leena*ji*.'

At that moment, I felt as if he was going to burst into tears, but thank God, he did not.

I wanted to tell him that *I am in no pain; in fact, I am absolutely fine.*

'I have seen my mother in pain when my father died. While growing up, I had decided that I would work hard and give a life of comfort to my mother and sister. I used to work for nearly fifteen hours a day. I sacrificed pleasure-time with friends and got my sister married in a good family.'

His syrupy words were getting irksome to my ears. Once again, I felt as if he would now break down, but thank goodness, he did not.

With one more large packet of saccharine tumbling out of his vocal chords, he continued, 'Leena*ji*, I have a deep connection with pain. My heart goes out to the children on the streets. I feel the pain of that man who sleeps without a sheet on a winter night. I feel wretched when I look at a helpless mother who begs on the street in order to feed her child. There is so much pain around us, Leena*ji*. Don't you agree?'

I kept a pillow on my mouth so that no sound came out of me. Either I would have burst into a laugh or into tears… I was confused. I wanted to spank him with a spatula and ask, *decide whether you want to be gloomy or sugary! This combination of being both at the same time is getting on to my nerves.*

Had he given me this kind of talk in person, don't know what would I have done? Rushed to a charitable organisation and surrendered everything?

He was unperturbed even when not a word came out of me. 'What is the meaning of our lives? What kind of quests are we on? I often wonder, Leena*ji*. All of us are living for our own selves. Nobody is concerned about the plight of the needy. There is so much poverty and starvation and pain in this world. This life seems meaningless until the moment when I look into the eyes of my three-year-old nephew. His innocent eyes are filled with compassion and purity.'

His words were wrenching my heart, as I tugged at it hard with my pillow. *Oh God, why had Bollywood not discovered him yet? He could be the ideal replacement for our very own Nirupa Roy! He could even direct a tear-jerker blockbuster depicting the squalor, poverty, pain and misery of the needy! It could probably win us an Oscar or two....*

'Oh, what did I start talking! You must be wondering that why am I speaking of the meaning of life when we are supposed to discuss each other. What interests you, Leena*ji,* if you may allow me to ask?'

There it goes...another pack of sugar emptied! His throat needed a CT scan! I must know what is inside and how can he talk so sweet all the time?

I was at a loss for words: *If I speak now of my desire to go to Switzerland or how I love to gobble chaat and mithai—he will probably have me guillotined—declaring me to be guilty of eking the morsels out of the mouth of those starving! He will be aghast if I now mention leisure and food, when there is so much pain in the world!*

I felt like a culprit.

'Leena*ji*... Leena*ji*, are you there?'

'I like to...errr... I... I like to...read and...and sleep... No, I meant....' *Am I crazy? What have I just said?* I regretted every word.

'Leena*ji*, we will all sleep forever, one day. This life is a book...every day a new chapter unfolds. Every day, life gives us a new reason to feel sad and then again, on its next page—there is a new reason to feel joyous.'

I heard a *sniff...sniff. Was it me or was he sobbing?*

After a long pause this time, he continued, 'Leena*ji*, how would you like to take this forward? May we speak again for a few times or do you think our elders should connect?'

'I will let you know, Shailesh. Ooops...Shailesh*ji*.'

'Thank you, Leena*ji*. May I request you to join me in a prayer for two minutes? Let us pray for less pain in our lives and in the lives of those around us and in our world.'

I wanted to take the bed-side lamp and bang my head with it! He did not wait for my reply.

He began to utter a prayer to the Almighty, asking Him to grant greater compassion and pity in our hearts, for our less-fortunate brothers and sisters!

I needed a catharsis! I wanted to scream…cry and howl on the top of my voice.

The next morning, at breakfast, Mom asked with concern, 'Binnie, why are your eyes red? Did you not sleep well? And why are you not eating the *aloo paranthas*? Shall I put a little more butter on them?'

I kept mum. I just could not eat. I could see Shailesh standing next to me, and peering at my *paranthas* with a look of sheer horror on his face and saying: *'How can you, Leenaji? How can you stuff yourself up with paranthas-topped-with-butter, when there are millions of children dying due to starvation every minute? Shame on you!'*

The Open-ended Episode

For the next few days, I could neither sleep and nor eat well. I had not connected with Shailesh*ji* again, after that one conversation. He must have been a nice fellow, but guess, I could not handle it all. He was too sweet and the excessive courteousness had driven me crazy in that one night.

I need a break… I got to do something different. May be join Zumba, or learn French? Naaahhh… Should I join ballet classes? Hmm… I was lost in thoughts when I heard Mom say, 'Binnie, do you know Kamini who lives in A block? Oh ho…the one who believes herself to be a culinary expert? The one who dresses and moves about seductively? Well, she is doing a workshop on "Learn to Cook the Thai Way" this Sunday. And, oh God! Do you know how much is she charging? How can the whole world think of making money only by fleecing others? To charge Rs 2,000 for three hours is sheer extortion, I am telling you. Unbelievable! I better watch *YouTube* and learn to cook Thai food!'

'A three-hour class on learning to make Thai food? Oh wow! Wonderful! I want to attend this workshop.'

Mom rolled her eyes for an instant and looked at me, bewildered. Noticing the firm intent on my face and enthusiasm in my voice, she decided to not argue further and replied, 'Very well, do as you feel like… I will forward her number to you.'

I excitedly messaged Chirag about it. For a change, he did not tell me in that sharp tone of his that: *you are wrong, Leena…* He egged me promptly and even joked about girls trying to learn cooking exotic foods, just so as to impress guys! I tried prying about what his rumoured girlfriend was trying to learn so as to impress him, but to no avail. I noticed that whenever I tried to ask him what exactly was happening in his personal life, he either evaded it smoothly or in that instant became guarded and defensive and refused to share anything. I was sure though that a girl had to be there somewhere….

At 11 am on Sunday, I reached Kamini's house with a pen and notepad in my hand. As I stepped in, I saw a table neatly set with induction gas, tools and Thai condiments. The aroma of spices had already filled the air and my hunger pangs were stimulated. I noticed that beside myself, there were two more attendees: Ekta, a yoga trainer who lived in our colony, and the omnipresent and omni-intrusive Mrs Sharma.

Wow...pupils are few and that implies more attention from the trainer and liberal portions of delicacies to taste, I thought and smiled.

Halfway through making green curry and lotus stem stew, Kamini gave the ladies a break of ten minutes. As we sat sipping lemongrass and citrus flavoured tea, Mrs Sharma looked at me in a queer way, while making no efforts to conceal the envy in her demeanour. *She seems to be thinking a thing or two about me. Hmm... What could it be?* I wondered. I did not have to wonder for long, as she spoke up herself.

'Leena, it is so nice to see you here, but I wonder why *you* are here? Why do you want to learn Thai cooking? Your Mom cooks well, isn't it? Or, are some bells ringing far away? *Oye hoye*...some secretttttt?'

'Oh no, Aunty*ji*... Nothing of the kind. I am just learning because I like Thai food,' I protested, feebly.

'*Arrey,* but why do you have to learn? You are a free bird! You don't have any commitments... No, of course, you may have some, I am sure. But nothing enforced on you. If you like something, you can do. If you don't like something, you just drop it and move on. Wish we too could do so... Don't you agree, Ekta*ji*? Why are you and I here? We are like caged birds. Our husbands get bored with what we cook every day for them, and see...here we are, learning how to cook the Thai way! In a few days, they will again make faces, and comment on our dull lives or on our unappetising cooking and off we shall trot, trying to learn how to apply make-up the French style or how to make things out of waste or how to stay in shape or how to cook the Mexican way. Isn't it? I am telling you, Leena, you are very lucky. Am I telling lies, Ekta Madam?' She gave a sharp look of *dare-you-challenge-me* to Ekta, and the poor soul nodded as sheepishly as a worried mouse would.

I could have kept quiet, had I been sane. However, I was obviously not. 'Aunty*ji*, just because I am single, it does not mean that I cannot upgrade my cooking skills. Actually, you are right, there is certainly a difference. I am here to learn for myself, while you are here to learn for someone else. I wonder if you live for yourself ever!'

There was fire in Mrs Sharma's eyes, as she looked at me in total contempt and I had to put up with her tart expressions for the rest of the workshop. Kamini, meanwhile, kept wondering what was it about the lemongrass and citrus flavoured tea that had led to expressions going sour! Nobody (except Kamini) spoke with anybody for the rest of the two hours. The silence was a bit uncomfortable, but it did not deter me from taking a double serving of delicacies we were taught to make. *Aha, the tom yum soup is something to die for, especially when accompanied with the delicious sweet corn cutlets,* I mumbled, heedless to the stares I was receiving as I gulped the food.

As soon as I entered home, Mom was all geared up to snatch my notepad and take a close look at the ingredients needed for the next day's culinary experiment. I happily gave away the notepad. Mom hurriedly made a list of the ingredients she needed and scooted to the market.

This Thai workshop was quite therapeutic and I must tell Chirag about it. I checked the World Clock on my mobile. *It is a bit too early there.* I waited for an hour and called him.

Besides the above, I also eagerly wanted to ask him about the keynote address he was to deliver at a prestigious university on the outskirts of the Silicon Valley, on the occasion of their week-long celebrations on Sustaining High Standards of Excellence in Academic Research. We went over the key points of his address and edited them a bit with his and mine inputs all falling into place together. And then, it was my turn to jibber-jabber. When I shared with him the glee that I experienced while giving the sharp reply to Sharma Aunty, we roared with laughter together. I had stopped feeling inhibited about sharing the silly titbits of day-to-day life with the busy and high-profiled guy that Chirag was.

By the time, we concluded our babble (from my end), two hours had passed and Mom had returned from shopping. The ingredients for the next day's to-be exotic Thai meal were all on her kitchen table!

I was checking the other messages of the day when a notification popped up, from *shaadi-ka-laddoo.com: 'We* have four new partner recommendations for you, Leena.'

I scanned the four profiles. After deleting the first three, I paused at the fourth one.

'Hi, I am Amit, a 40-year-old Punjabi guy based in Canada for more than 21 years. I hold an M.Sc. from Punjab University and I work as a medical transcriptionist. There is my father, an elder brother, his wife and their two kids in my family and they are based in Chandigarh. Divorced twice, details can be shared later. I am simple, God-fearing, and a vegetarian. I love to read spiritual and inspirational books and watch movies during my free time. Thank you for reading on me.'

I felt a positive vibe as I scrolled through Amit's picture and profile. *Looks simple and elegant with a smile on his face*—I thought and mused on whether to send him an Invite to connect. I sat with my eyes closed, trying to listen to my inner voice. The heart said *yes* and I did....

Two days later, I received a forwarded message from Mom stating Amit's acceptance of the Invite to connect. The message contained his mobile number and an admonishing one-liner from Mom that read: 'Now don't take ages to make the next move. Send him a WhatsApp message now.'

I looked at the watch. *There is still time before I go to sleep and it must be day-time in Canada.*

Hi Amit,

This message is in response to your profile on *shaadi-ka-laddoo.com*

Let us chat sometime to proceed further.

Thank You, Leena

After 15 minutes:

Hi Leena,

Thanks for sending the message. Can we connect in about ten minutes?

I replied: 'Yes, sure.'

An international number flashed on my phone after ten minutes. I took the call and a very soft-spoken and amiable voice greeted me from the other end.

'Hi Leena, this is Amit here. Hope you are free to talk.'

'Hey Amit, how are you? Yes, we can talk.'

'I just finished making my breakfast and lunch, and I can chat comfortably now.'

'Oh, don't you have to rush for work?'

In a very relaxed tone, Amit said, 'No, I do an afternoon to late night shift. I still have about three hours before I leave home.'

'You are a medical transcriptionist?' I was puzzled.

'Well, Leena, I was a medical transcriptionist for almost eight years, until last year. Due to prolonged sitting for nearly 10-11 hours, I developed a hand tendon issue and suffered from an agonising backache. The doctor advised me that unless I changed the kind of work I was doing, surgery would become imminent,' he explained.

'Oh, then?' I wondered where this was going.

Amit continued, 'Well, I had to quit then and now I work with a security firm. I manage the Accounts there. Though I took a hit on my salary, the job is less strenuous and the work hours are less demanding too.'

Though I felt a bit uneasy about the difference between what he was actually doing and what was posted on his profile, I decided not to dismiss him too soon. He seemed to have read my mind.

'Leena, I know you are thinking about the contrast between what is written on my profile and what I exactly do. You can choose to disconnect anytime.

I know I should have updated my profile by now but am a little hesitant as yet. However, when someone responds to the profile and I happen to connect with that person, I share the detail about this change in the kind of work I do, at the very outset.'

'Okay, Amit. I am fine. Let us talk further.'

He seems sincere and if he had to change his work due to health reasons, and was reluctant to announce it to the world, let me not hold that against him, I decided.

'Thank you, Leena. For this year I have decided to go on with the low profile, nurse myself to good health and then I shall look for a better-paying job towards the end of the year.'

'Best wishes for your health, Amit. Tell me more about yourself. Your interests, goals, family—just about anything you may want to share.'

The talk was, so far, comfortable. There was nothing freakish or awkward about him.

'I have been in Canada for over twenty-one years. I had left India when I was barely 20 years old. Came here, picked up a few odd jobs and then finally settled as a medical transcriptionist. In those days, opportunities in India were not in abundance as they are now. Every house in Punjab dreamt of sending at least one member or as many as possible to the US or to Canada. My father too was determined to send me to either of the two countries. My mother passed away when I was about five years old. My brother and I are very close to our father and he has raised us in a disciplined way. So, that is about me. Hmm, what else? I live in a rented apartment, have a few friends and relatives whom I visit sometimes. I practise yoga and like to watch movies, and love to read biographies of saints and leaders. Guess that is a lot about me.'

'That is nice. Yoga interests me too. I am a certified trainer and do conduct sessions with a cross-section of the society. I am a lecturer in a college here and it is a full-time job. I plan my yoga sessions in advance therefore, and generally schedule them in the evenings. I live with my parents and younger brother and I love travelling.'

Amit and I spoke about yoga, books and our future goals that night. The talk concluded without any commitment of speaking the next day or in the next few days. Nothing much was amiss, but a few doubts nevertheless lingered... *I think he suppresses his opinions. He became cautious every time he mentioned his father. He did not seem to like living in Canada much... Why then does he not return to India? Guess, he is apprehensive of his father's reaction to such a decision. And ah, I forgot... He has had two marriages already. What must have gone wrong? Twice?*

Amit and I started connecting every 3-4 days. It neither seemed as if the talks were leading us anywhere and nor they seemed driven by any pressure or a purpose. We kind of liked it that way. However, I did subtly try to speak about his father and about his covert desire to move back to India, but received a feeble response every time.

For three weeks, there was not a word by either of us about our respective earlier marriages. One day, he finally spoke up, 'Leena, I have been married twice. I know it is quite intimidating for a girl to even consider such a proposal but what I liked about you is that you did not question me about it and nor did you attempt probing into the matter. I feel comfortable now to talk about the failed marriages with you.'

I braced myself for it, though not eagerly. I said, 'Okay.'

'My first wife belonged to a small town in Punjab. We were married young under parental pressure. She was not educated and I did not have the courage to question my father's decision. She came with me to Canada and three months later, she made it known that she was going to take up a job. She picked up a sales job at a store and she was smart at it. It took her one year to learn the nuances of the work. She began to earn very well; she was tipped well and she even began to have casual flirtations with other men.

Within the next year and a half, she became a different person altogether. I was conscious of her changing hues, but decided to remain quiet so as to have peace at home. She did not harbour any such intention, though. One day, she came home and declared upfront that she was leaving me and the house. I tried to reason with her, but nothing worked. She said she was in love with someone else and that she needed a divorce. Even after she left home, some of our relatives who live here, tried to talk sense into her but to no avail. Eventually, we separated legally. And…my father…he….'

I could hear a muffled sob. He was finding it difficult to go on. 'It is okay. You need not tell me everything… It is absolutely fine.'

Amit took a moment or two to compose himself.

'No, I am good… It happened long ago. Whenever I recollect how my father was upset with me because my wife left me for someone else, it is his rebuke that hurts me more than anything else. I did not visit India for the next three years.'

A pause ensued. I did not want to know details of his second marriage. It was sufficient food-for-thought for a night. He wished to continue, though.

'In those three years, my father sent me a few proposals but nothing clicked. Then I happened to meet a Punjabi girl, here in Canada. Her parents were from Chandigarh. We fell in love and told our families and married soon thereafter. All was well for about two years until one day I realised that she was sending a lot of money to her parents in India. Whenever I asked her about it, she vehemently denied. After a couple of months, she began to insist on calling her brother to Canada for work. She wanted him to come and stay with us. In fact, she wanted her entire family to come and live with us. This time around, I mustered the courage to tell her that it was unacceptable to me. After all, we were happy together—just the two of us. I did not want to complicate it all, by bringing families into our home. She refused to budge from her wish and our verbal spats became frequent and ugly. The stalemate turned bitter by the day and after about six months, we separated and she moved to another city. I had to pay heavily for this second-time, short-term marital experiment. She got away with a hefty alimony.'

Saying so, he once again retreated into silence. I waited for him to speak. I did not have anything to say. It would have been terrible to offer sympathetic words at that juncture....

After a few moments, he resumed, 'My last two experiences were quite traumatic but now I am open to new possibilities. I want to settle down, and have kids.'

'I am sorry to hear about the way your previous marriages turned out but again, life always gives another chance.'

'Yes, I so very much wish to return to India, work in Chandigarh and settle down there but my father…,' Amit trailed off.

Another pause followed, and this time, a long one. I felt I was in no position to say anything to him. If he desired for something and could not have it because of his father's authoritarian ways, well…he had to sort it all out.

After that day, both of us did not connect for two weeks. I was relieved for it gave me the much-needed breather to think it through. Mom knew about Amit and wanted to call his father in order to fix a date for meeting up. I wasn't sure though. *Amit is a nice guy…simple and modest too. What is it that is bothering me then? Perhaps, the lack of courage in him to stand up for himself and his happiness. What if he always remains thus? Whenever I think of him, a cowered and meek image comes to mind. And, who knows the extent to which his personality is bruised by his father's smothering ways,* I wondered. *Possibly, something about him and his father could have pushed his previous wives away from him.*

Mom was keen to take up the matter further with his father. She was clueless about his father's ways and the hold that he had had over his children's lives. The Universe connives in its own ways though, beyond what we can fathom. Two weeks stretched into a month, and my speculations and even Mom's queries subsided after a while.

One fine day, I received a message from Amit:

'Hey Leena, it was nice connecting with you. I wish you luck.'

There were no definitive questions and no explicit answers. I smiled.

'Likewise for you, Amit,' I replied.

The Miscellaneous

Case 1

Arindam, First Officer, Merchant Navy.
Mumbai.

Trin... Trin... Trin...

Me: 'Hello.'

(Pleasantries are exchanged...usual drill is repeated.)

Thereafter,

Arindam: 'I sail for six months in a year and I want to get married before I go out to the sea again. By the way, I live in a rented apartment and my mother lives just two houses away from mine. She takes care of my house in my absence. Hope you don't mind that. It happens that girls, at first, tell that they don't mind but then, later they raise a furore over one thing or the other. Hence, when I state the facts before you—do tell me upfront. I am a flexible person, though.'

Me: Huh? I don't think that any of it matters....'

Arindam: 'By the way, I was just testing you. I own my house but don't disclose it upfront to prospective alliances. They may think—"Oh, he is a marine guy…must be loaded with money." I am not looking for someone who is after my money. Leena, you have cleared my test!'

Me: 'Thank you.'

I wanted to add: *Yes, I have never felt this triumphant ever since I had cleared my Class X Board exams.*

Arindam: 'Should I then fly down to see you? It will be good to meet your family too. I leave in two months. We can get engaged at least, before I sail.'

Me (startled): 'This is too soon. I don't think hurrying in this matter is a good idea.'

We have not even seen each other…never spoken before and he is scheduling our engagement according to his calendar?

Arindam: 'Tell you what… I can postpone my sailing to after three months. Should I fly down in July? My mother too loves Delhi and all the shopping and eating outlets there, especially the *chaat* corners!'

Oh God, he is choking me!

Me: 'I got to go now. Thank you for your time.'

Arindam: 'Okay, let me know. I am flexible with sailing. Is it okay with you if I don't wish you *good morning* and *good night* every day, when I join the ship? Sometimes, we don't get the network but I will try my best….'

Me (hurriedly): 'Okay, bye.'

Six months and ten days later, a message in the *shaadi-ka-laddoo.com* chat box:

Arindam: 'Logged in to delete my account. Am already married…it happened a month after we spoke. And, ha…ha…ha… You still looking around? Very sad, eh?'

Case 2

Abhishek, Software Engineer at TMS.

Bengaluru.

On Viber:

Me: 'I read your travel blog, Abhishek. It is quite cool. Do you trek every weekend?'

Abhishek: 'Hi Leena, thank you. Yes, I trek and travel as much as I can, and usually all by myself. I am basically happy in my own company. I visit my parents 3-4 times in a year, and they live in our ancestral house in a far-off village, 300 km from Bengaluru. I cook my own food, watch movies alone and I am preparing myself for the Ladakh Half Marathon.'

An obvious thought came to my mind: *Why are you on shaddi-ka-laddoo.com*?

Me: 'Adventure seems to be running in your veins.'

Abhishek: 'Yes, I love photography too. I can be with my lens for hours. I don't need and like anything or anyone in those hours.'

Another obvious thought: *Is there room for anyone else in your life?*

But I could think of nothing to say to him.

Abhishek: 'Leena, it is now time for my run. Catch you later. Do read my new blog on the Coorg Forest.'

Without waiting for my reply, he disconnected.

Two days later:

Abhishek (a message on Skype): 'Hey Leena, it was nice to connect but I didn't get the vibes to take it further. Good luck!'

Me (in my head): *What?*

Goodbye, Abhishek.

Case 3

Mohit, Stock Analyst. Father of two (kids live with their mother) wonderful girls.

Calgary, Canada.

One Phone Call + One Video Call + WhatsApp chats

Scene 1

Mohit: 'Hey Leena, my kids are aged eight and four years respectively. It is very important for me to have someone who can accept my children and give them love. They are an extension of me. My weekends are for my children. I hope you are fine with that.'

Me: 'Hi Mohit, I guess we can talk on this matter later. It is too soon. I liked your profile and would like to know a bit more about you. I read and I know that you have kids. When we accept a person in our life, we accept all their loved ones too.'

Scene 2

Mohit: 'Leena, do you like shopping?'

Guys! Guys! You guys never stop amazing me! Now, what kind of a question is this? And, you are asking this to a girl? With someone you have interacted for barely 2-3 minutes?

Me: 'No, I do not enjoy shopping.'

I hope I too have now shocked you, ha…ha….

Mohit: 'I had a very painful marriage and then, an ugly divorce. She was a shopaholic, and an alcoholic. I used to always find her either in the shopping malls or in the pubs. Somehow, I don't trust women when they say that they don't like shopping. The basic psyche of women is ultimately the same.'

Scene 3 (on video call)

Mohit: 'You look so beautiful, Leena. I feel you are a balanced woman and I must say, you don't look your age.'

Me (to myself): *Whoa! Am I supposed to dance with joy on hearing this? Ever since I have registered on this site that allures all with a shaadi-ka-laddoo, I feel like I am permanently stationed on a rollercoaster ride.*

Me: 'It was nice speaking with you, Mohit. Let us talk a few more times and then see.'

Two days later: On WhatsApp...

Me: 'Hi Mohit, hope you had a good weekend with your little girls.'

Mohit: 'Yes.'

Me: 'How is everything?'

Mohit: 'Fine.'

Me: 'What's new?'

Mohit: 'Nothing.'

Conversation ends.

That night, message on WhatsApp:

Mohit: 'You came across as a very sweet girl, Leena. I liked talking to you but on second thoughts, I think you are too young to handle my kids. Take care.'

Case 4

Unnamed Guy, Established Professional.

Cannot disclose country of residence.

An e-mail:

Hi Leena,

I know you will be surprised to receive this e-mail from me. For reasons which I cannot disclose, am unable to tell you my name and other details. However, please do not view this mail with suspicion or even consider it as spam. I am settled outside India and have come to know about you through some sources. I know a few details about you; have gone through your profile on *shaadi-ka-laddoo.com* and have heard someone talk about you. Based on all of it, I liked you and your profile/interests.

I just want to know a little more about you, before I tell you about myself. Will it be possible for you to trust this mail, coming from a total stranger, and reply to me? I assure you sincerely that this is no prank and there is no hidden ulterior motive either.

Will you please share with me your views on life in general, and on marriage, in particular? Do you look at marriage as a necessity because it is difficult to live life alone? I understand that this will be your second marriage. Even after one experience having gone wrong earlier, are you prepared to enter into wedlock once again, with total faith and hope? Will you not be cautious and guarded? Will you not be wary of placing your trust in another man and in this institution once again?

I am sorry to ask you these many questions, but it is important for me to know your views on trust, compatibility, commitment and so on. Do you look at marriage as a commitment-for-lifetime? Or, a mutually convenient arrangement so that life becomes smooth and easy to live? Hope you are not thinking of me as one old and harsh schoolmaster who is standing with a cane in his hand, and demanding answers. ☺

You are absolutely free to choose whether to answer to this mail, or otherwise. If you can trust me, please write what you feel about yourself and about life and people and about relationships. Please feel free to pen down whatever comes to your mind. Even if you wish to reprimand me for encroaching on your space without your prior consent, please do so. You can pretend that you are talking with yourself or pouring yourself out on a diary.

Will await your mail/reply with bated breath,

Unnamed Guy.

I was sitting in the college library when I read the mail. I was startled and at a loss for words. *Who could it be? A laddoo who has decided to remain anonymous and start the communication in a novel style? Or, is he someone I know who is playing a prank?* I was excited and surprised, both. *Should I reply? He seems to be harmless… But, NO! Let me think it over or consult someone and then reply. Could it be a hacker or someone intending harm?* All kinds of thoughts were resonating in my mind. I could not sit in the library and focus on the book at hand.

I left for home and wondered whether I should discuss this with either Chirag or Mom. I let go of the idea to speak with Mom, because she could/would blow the thing out of proportion. *It will be best to deal with it at my level or at best, to consult a confidante,* I decided.

A Sweet Little Something

One day, I returned home from college, only to find another bizarre episode waiting to unfold. I kept my bags and files on the table, and hit the bed. *Yaouch…* I shrieked in pain as my head hit something hard. I rubbed my head and sought to recover the cause of the thud. *Oh no! What on earth is this now*! I exclaimed holding a small cooking pan in my hand, kept underneath the pillow on the bed.

'MOM, please come over here…,' I called out.

'What happened, *beta*? Why are you sounding furious?' Mom had said *beta* a little too lovingly and that did ring a bell in my head.

She saw the cooking pan in my hand and a quizzical look on my face. For a second, she looked sheepish but then she immediately swerved towards her bold and undaunted (the usual) expression and said, 'Oh, this is for your good, dear. You know….'

Before she could complete her sentence, I interrupted with a force. 'I do not know anything, Mom, and I do not wish to know anything! It is getting too freakish now. I agreed to that whole marrying-the-pot thing but why have you now kept a cooking pan under my pillow? Wasn't the pot supposed to bring me a groom?' I asked, indignantly.

'Binnie,' Mom held my arm and while making me sit on the bed, said in her politest, best tone, 'You see dear, these astrological remedies take time. Mrs Kukreja made her son feed a cow every morning at five for a month as told by *Pandit* Dilbhara*ji*, and the boy finally met the girl of his dreams on Day 32. Mark my words—there is lot of potency in what *Panditji* says.'

'Why bring this *Panditji* again into the picture? Didn't Mr Sharma, the palmist friend of Papa give the idea of marrying a clay pot? What if the pot clashes with the pan thing?' and saying so, I gave a sarcastic laugh, despite the annoying situation.

Mom could barely suppress her own temptation to laugh. 'I think Mr Sharma is not devoting too much time to his practice now. He is becoming old. Not everything he has prophesied has actually happened. We must try at all levels, my dear,' and saying so, she tucked the cooking pan firmly underneath the pillow, patted my back and left the room.

I resigned, and this time—gently placed my head on the pillow.

The next day, I decided to try something different. I decided to pamper myself with the luxury of being driven to work. I wanted to put ear-plugs, enjoy music, shut the world out and relax for an hour or so. I booked a pool-cab ride for myself.

I settled into the backseat, and closed my eyes, while humming to myself. There was another girl (in her late twenties, it seemed) already seated and engaged on the phone, sharing the ride. She was quiet for the first few seconds and apparently, the person at the other end was doing the talking. One minute later, I came to know that she was pretty badly hassled in life. The words fell on my ears, without much ado. 'Mom, let me reach office. Please give me…like 25 minutes, at least. I am not flying to work here… I am stuck in traffic. Please, Mom… I will reach office and send you the edited profile. What is the emergency?' She went silent once again. *Guess, must be receiving flak from the other end,* I was amused. And then, it was the daughter's turn once again, 'Mom, are you implying that if I don't send my profile in the next two minutes, then all the boys registered on *mere-jeevan-saathi.com* will fling the garland onto other necks and whoosh, be gone? Phew! Yes…yes… I had been up last night and have re-done my profile. Yes, have added the detail about how much I love large, joint families,' and saying so, she disconnected the line and let out a deep sigh. She looked towards me, gave me a wry smile and turned away her face without waiting to acknowledge one from me.

Are all the girls in their late twenties and thirties single and searching for grooms and are all the mothers going about playing dog-and-the-bone in frenzy? Why the rush? Guess, only mothers would know! During the next 30 minutes or so, the ride was calm—other than the usual melee caused by the congestion on the roads.

During break-time in college, my phone rang. An unknown number flashed on the screen. I took the call and there was a: 'Hey, Leena,' from the other end.

'Hi, may I know who this is?'

'Leena, this is me... Vishal.'

'Vishal?' *Do I know any Vishal?* I asked myself.

'Oh, okay! It seems you have not recognised me. Let me remind you... We met last year during the inter-collegiate debate at the Annual Youth Meet in Jaipur. I was there representing the HRD Ministry and we were together on one of the panel discussions.'

I recollected immediately. 'Oh, yes... Hi Vishal! It's been a long time.'

A bubble appeared in my head picturing Vishal: *bony, tall, fair, smartly attired in a cotton kurta and torn jeans and always carried with him an air of exuberance.*

He was a good debater too. I had had many a hearty laughs as he never did let go of any opportunity to put the moderators and fellow panellists, including me, in a spot with his witty remarks. He reminded me of Shahid Kapoor.

'Yes, what a discussion that was and thereafter, we had one intense debate over coffee.'

'Yes, I cannot forget that either. It was such a quick meeting and connection with you and then silence for one full year.'

'I know… I should have also made an effort to connect, Vishal.'

'Likewise. I was just clearing up my old e-mails and I glanced at one of yours which had your phone number. I thought—let me make a fresh start.'

'That is one fabulous thing you have done this year,' I said and we both laughed aloud.

'Want to have one debate over coffee again, Leena?'

'Sure, why not? Let me call you next week and we shall finalise the day and time.'

Vishal had turned out to be one of those *out-of-sight; out-of-mind* cases. I remembered that he was a charming, intellectually sound and a humble person and was nearly the same age as me. *And yes, I remember that he too loved travelling.*

I called him next week, and we decided to meet one Saturday afternoon at Barista in Connaught Place at 4 pm.

'Hi Leena!' Vishal was beaming.

We shook hands, and our elation was absolutely mutual.

'Must say, better late than never. It feels great to meet you again,' I replied.

'Yes, indeed.'

We both settled for cappuccinos and impending talks at a corner table.

'So, how have you been, Leena?'

'Life has been good—in fact, has been wrapped up with lectures, reading, writing, yoga, and travels. How about you?'

'Well, I completed the project I was working on for the HRD Ministry and I am now working as a management consultant with a finance company. Otherwise, mostly at home.'

'That is cool. So, what inspired you to re-connect?' I was inquisitive.

'Honestly, I was quite impressed with you the first time we met. I had liked your passion for travel and your commitment towards your students and yoga and also your strong opinions when we had our own monologue-kind of a debate,' he laughed aloud yet again. 'But, I got so very entangled with the project

I was handling for the Ministry that a year passed by in a flash. Since the past two months, I have been planning to call you and meet you.'

'Planning to meet up for any specific reason or for just a casual chat?' I did not give up digging for the real reason.

'Well, one fine day, I thought of travelling solo this year, and at that very moment, I thought of you... I said to myself—who better than Leena to become my travel guru!' Vishal said with a broad grin.

'Hey... Hey, no... No. I am no travel guru... I had just shared with you some of my travelogues and escapades but where do you intend to rush off to?'

'I am chalking out a plan to explore Thailand, Vietnam and Cambodia in depth—over two months.'

'Wow! That is indeed brave, Vishal.'

'Don't know as yet. If you remember, though I love exploration and adventure, I have hitherto always travelled either for work, or typically as a tourist—and just got an overview of a place in a day or two. A tentative plan of this kind was simmering in my mind for over two years, but perhaps it will now finally see light at the end of the tunnel.'

'Why do you say *perhaps*? It is a fantabulous plan! Go ahead! Do it, Vishal,' I cheered.

We discussed the history and geography, and the interesting tales about the people of these Far East

Asian nations. We discussed the terrific storehouse of information that the *Lonely Planet*'s travel guides for Vietnam, Cambodia, and Northern Thailand were… We counted the funny the pros and cons of living single and travelling solo and we even seriously contemplated the prospect of enrolling for an interesting academic program and continuing to study further.

As he booked a cab for home, I was surprised that he did not have a car. I did not ask him anything but noticing the quizzical look on my face, he explained everything.

'No, I don't have a car. I don't drive and I don't intend to buy a car. You see, Leena, I am a very need-based person who believes in minimalist living. I like to keep my life hassle-free. Fewer materialistic possessions, less complicated relationships—and the result is less stress. I am 35 years old, not married, and living with my sister who is 45 and has also chosen to remain single. We both share our monthly expenses and are living a peaceful, simple life.'

Though it was unusual to hear about minimalist living from a new-age, young, working professional who lived in a superfluous metro city, I was intrigued by Vishal's views on living life the modest way. *He dares to think differently!*

He was in the mood to share further, 'I want to study further, Leena. Perhaps, I will take up a certificate course in the Brahmi script or a Diploma in Indian Culture and History.'

'Wow, planning to learn a new script at 35! Don't you face pressure from your parents to marry when, at your age, most men have two kids and a big belly and all that they think of is making their fat packages a little fatter! They are obsessed with the bullish trends on the stock-market and afraid of their own and their family's rising health-care bills. You are certainly one odd man out,' I said with a visible look of admiration.

'Ha! Ha! Ha! Yes, I am odd. My parents did try their best to *normalise* me until about two years ago when they realised that this guy is no ordinary case. My sister too, thinks alike. We both decided to rent an apartment for ourselves in order to keep peace with our parents, though we visit them every now and then. We divide our days of cooking, cleaning and other household chores. She has her own circle of friends, and I have mine.'

I was all ears as he continued: 'I believe life is given to us to live. It is not to be spilled and frittered away, particularly in trying to please others. There is much to learn and grow from day-to-day experiences. And each one must decide what makes him or her truly content and relaxed and have the wisdom and courage to precisely do that. Just as I love to travel, read, and make new friends—so also, each one must choose one's own path. If one is happy with hoarding and heftier balances in the bank, one must do that. Don't you think so, Leena?'

He is so different from the usual lot! No wonder, I couldn't find anyone like him on shaadi-ka-laddoo.com, I concluded, nonchalantly.

'Have you never felt a void, as far as companionship is concerned?' I wanted to know how he coped with that.

'Of course, I would love to share my life with a person who can add meaning and joy to it... I would love to date someone, Leena. There were a few relationships in the past and although they were wonderful as such, but I felt stifled soon. What about you? What is your mantra of life?'

I felt that he had spoken my mind already. My own views on life resonated in Vishal's words. *Well, almost....*

The cab had taken 15 minutes to arrive, and I thanked the traffic for that! We parted ways with a to-be-continued look in our eyes. I could sense a soft little corner developing in my heart.

I was eager to meet him one more time. The next weekend, I buzzed Vishal.

'Hey, do you want to catch the new satirical stand-up comedy at Akshara Theatre on Sunday?'

'Whoopeee! It sounds interesting... What time?'

'At 7 pm.'

'Done! Will you meet me at the metro station? We can walk together to the theatre.'

'Done,' I smiled while replying.

Sunday was a fine day, as good as it could get. The walk to the theatre was pleasing. Our mutter of amusement blossomed into an enormous belly-laugh in the theatre. On my way home, I was pretty convinced that Vishal is not a run-of-the-mill sort of guy. He is different... He seems so carefree when he talks. No hang-ups at all.

Over the next six weeks, I was busy every weekend, enjoying theatre shows, coffee chats and strolls with Vishal. There appeared a silver lining to my otherwise dread for Sundays. I was particularly comfortable with the non-committal and tag-free meet-ups with Vishal. There was no pressure to impress or to be correct and nice.

We were walking aimlessly one evening at Lodhi Garden when he asked, 'Hey Leena, are you free to meet this coming Sunday?'

'Yes, why?'

'Don't know if you will be interested... There is a cultural fest showcasing the art and culture from our North-Eastern States at the India Habitat Centre. I would love to see it.'

'Oh, wonderful… Count me in! And thereafter, *sevpuri* at Bengal Sweet Corner?'

'Perfect. I am game for it.'

We were acting like chirpy teenagers did when planning their evenings with buddies.

The showcasing of art and culture from the Seven Sisters was spell-binding. *Does all of it appeal more because I am here with Vishal?* I chose to ignore my own question.

We swooped at Bengal Sweet Corner and ordered 3-4 varieties of *chaat,* including *sevpuri.*

And then, as we were gulping down mouthful of *dahi-bhalle,* Vishal broke the news. Or, was it my heart that I heard breaking with a *boom boom ba-dum tssshhhhh!*

'Leena, have to tell you something. There is a change in plans.'

'What plans?'

'Not going to Thailand anymore.'

'Okay?'

He stopped eating and focused on what he had to say. I continued savouring.

'Well, I have been writing to universities across the world for a few months now and sending my applications. I got a call from the Bond University in Berlin. I have secured a part scholarship deal for a two-year course in Understanding Culture and Art in Europe during the Byzantine period. It starts in August—three months from now. I will manage the remaining fee with my savings and a little help from my father.'

This time, the *sevpuri* crumbled in my fingers... I was not sure if I was to look happy or sad. 'But you never mentioned that you have been applying to universities. I do remember though, that you told me about your desire to study further.'

'Yes, I refrained from discussing the applications part because nothing was certain. Till date, all the universities had been rejecting my application, probably because I sought assistance and scholarships. This one has come as a surprise. Leena, I am truly happy. I am so looking forward to exploring Europe, the academic way.'

I tried not to look crestfallen. 'How long will you be gone? I shall miss you, my friend.' My voice, nevertheless, shook as I spoke.

'Well, the course is for a year and a half, and thereafter, I will have to work on my dissertation. I may stay back for some more time and try to secure some assignments or work related to the course or may enrol for a Ph.D. I can't say anything for sure, as of now. And anyway, I have no strings attached anywhere. I am a free bird. Let's see where this course and this life take me from here.'

I have no strings attached—his words kept ringing in my ears. *Why am I feeling bad? Perhaps because it is as if one moment I have a friend with whom there is no pretence and the next moment, he is gone. Both of us were unattached with any strings,* I nudged myself.

'Vishal, congratulations! This is terrific news. Do not forget to explore as much as you can—both, Eastern and Western Europe while at the University. You do not have much time left… You may have to do packing and even reading up a bit for the course. By the way, would you like to take a look at a book I remember having read once and it is in our library—on the Macedonian Renaissance, during the 10th and 11th centuries when the Byzantine Empire really expanded quite strongly?'

'Yes! Much needs to be done. And, the book will be a great help. I will surely return it to you before I leave.'

That evening, we bid goodbye a little poignantly as if we both knew that it was going to be a long time before we met again…or never again, perhaps? *Was it a coincidence that we both took the metro back home in opposite directions,* I wondered ruefully.

The Beginning

Vishal left for Germany and my life was back on track in a few days. I wrapped up the little and sweet memories, along with my good wishes and bundled them all with him, as he departed.

Mom remained absorbed in seriously scanning the profiles at *shaadi-ka-ladoo.com* and forwarding a few to me with an amazing sense of regularity. *Mom's perseverance is splendid,* I often admitted to myself. She never gave up, and once in a while, her optimism rubbed off to me, as well. Otherwise, I had my emotional highs and lows with a regularity that matched with Mom's.

Shaurya and I were playing Scrabble one cool and breezy evening when there was a tinkle on the mobile, notifying an e-mail. A fierce competition was on and each, with clenched teeth, was determined to outdo the other. I decided to check the mail later. After my intelligent kid brother defeated me in the wordplay, I picked up the cell to check the few messages and the mail.

It was from the same e-mail ID, and from the person who had chosen to not name himself. *Oh no!*

I completely forgot about this guy! Well, his mail was a decent one but I was supposed to decide whether to send a reply or not, I recollected.

The mail read:

Hi once again,

How are you, Leena? I was not exactly expecting a reply from you, but then I was also not completely devoid of hope either. I checked my mail every day, fervently wishing....

I understand it is not easy to reply to a stranger, and more so, if the matter at hand is a personal one. However, I do earnestly urge you to write to me—at least, once. I need to know a bit about your present state of mind. Are you indeed serious about marrying again? Will you be doing so, without any baggage; without fears and insecurities?

I am also contemplating marriage and I like you, based on the little that I know about you. I am a little hesitant in picking up the phone and talking directly on the subject, as I would first like to know what you feel about the entire package deal that marriage is.

Will you trust this mail? Will you take a chance and respond to this message that destiny has placed in your inbox?

I will be delighted if you do,

Unnamed Guy.

Who is this guy? Who can he be? Why is he so scared to reveal his identity? Hmm, I must now decide whether to ignore the mail or reply to him. I mulled over.

For the next two days, I remained unsure and then finally, decided to ask Chirag about it. The next day, Chirag called and amongst other things, I told him about Vishal leaving for Germany and about this mail. He was quiet for a while and then he said in his typical gracious style, 'Do not ask me, Leena; ask your heart and do as it says.'

I decided to respond to the mail but in a guarded sort of way. *Who knows who is at the other end? If I ask Mom, she will raise brouhaha over it and never let me reply.*

I wrote:

Hi Unnamed Guy,

Although I have taken weeks to respond to your mail, the delay is not entirely owing to me being in a dilemma over it. Of course, I was in a bit of a spot, but I had also been preoccupied with a lot many things in this past one month. Now, when I have decided to reply to you—I am being guided by the heart, rather than by the rational mind.

I do not know who you are and how much do you know about me. I was married once, and am single now. I had liked that phase as much as I like this phase of my life. I never felt then that I had lost my freedom or space and nor do I feel now that I am lonely and desperately need a companion. I largely accept what comes my way. If I find a suitable person with whom life can be more joyous and fulfilling, it is fine and if I do not find one, it is absolutely fine too.

I will be lying if I say that I have no hurtful memories but they are just there; they do not haunt me and they will certainly not mar the days ahead. About what kind of a person I will be comfortable with, I am sorry but I would not share all of that with someone whose identity I know not.

Whoever you are, I hope I shall get to know soon. Meanwhile, my best wishes to you….

Leena.

I was satisfied with what I had written, for it was neither a brusque and nor a *too-revealing* kind of a reply.

The next day, our Principal summoned me and three other faculty members to his room and apprised us with the proposal approved by the management for organising the 'Start-Up 2.0 Conference' this year. I was baffled…*a year has passed since the conference last year?* Robert Orben's inspiring quote flashed before my eyes: *'Time flies. It's up to you to be the navigator.'* Discussions and conflicting opinions ensued amongst all present in the meeting and then with an indulgent smile, the Principal declared that I was to be the Convener this year as well. I was happy, but a groan escaped my throat—visualising the heavy load of responsibilities that the title entailed.

I came home and looking at my downcast face, Mom enquired what the matter was. I told her about the conference, and she was jubilant.

'Oh ho, Binnie, what is the matter with you? Such a respectable responsibility has been entrusted to you and it is because you did so well the last time. I am so happy, *beta*! Regarding the tremendous work that you shall have—why don't you give some of your tasks to me to handle?' she confidently demanded. I looked up at her with a look that said *Mom, you are unbelievable*!

'Why? What is the matter? You think I can't do what you can do? Rubbish! Of course, I can make calls on your behalf, and prepare lists of invitees and get your files and printouts ready. And oh, I can also prepare the menu of refreshments and meals for you. Just leave it all to me.' Mom was super-excited.

'Mommmmm, please…slow down! I will manage it… You do not worry and if I need your help, I will certainly ask you for it,' and I sat down on the chair with a sense of weariness enveloping me all around.

My eyes were closed when I heard Mom's voice, 'Binnie, sit up dear… Here, have this cup of hot chocolate with baked and salt-free chips. You will feel better.'

I was overwhelmed with her care and concern. I looked at her tenderly, got up and hugged her tight, and murmured, 'Mom, I love you indeed… You are the best Mom in the whole world.'

Papa also joined in and the three of us were sipping hot chocolate in a relaxed sort of way, when Mom exclaimed, '*Beta*, will Chirag be coming for the conference this year too? It was for a conference on similar lines that he had come and met you last year, isn't it? Well, this time, do remind him that he has to come home for lunch or dinner, and if he is bringing his family along, then they too are invited.'

I sat upright, and as if a magic wand had been waved, the heaviness vanished. *Oh, wow! Why did I not think of this? Of course, Chirag will be here, and we will meet after a year! Now, this is going to be exciting.* In an instant, I was all charged-up and looked forward to the preparations, the details and the responsibilities with a new-found enthusiasm.

Over the next one week, the Working Committee finalised the format of the conference and we began attending to the nitty-gritty. Work was underway with full gusto and the fervour was infectious. It had spread to all in the campus. The teaching and the non-teaching support staff, along with the students were all geared up for making the event a grand success! Once the list of keynote speakers and discussants and those who would be chairing sessions was finalised, I sat down with the list of names and their telephone numbers and of course, called Chirag first.

'Hey Chirag, how have you been?'

'Aha, Leena! Finally, I get to hear your voice. Where have you been? No call for more than a fortnight now? This is unacceptable! I object...,' Chirag answered in his usual, cheerful tone.

'Okay, I am pulling my ears here...,' I said with a ready laugh. 'Sorry, I could not call you since three weeks. It was all rush-rush here. Are you getting ready to go to work? I will just take a minute. We are organising the Start-up Conference once again this year in our college. You are cordially invited and as the Convener, I insist that you have to come.'

'Hold on, hold on... Am I rushing to work or are you rushing off somewhere? First, congratulations! Hurray! It is great that you shall be convening the conference yet again this year. I am sure it will be as or even more wonderful than last time.'

I interrupted him before he could finish. 'Chirag, why don't you take 3-4 days off your work so that you have some extra days here, after the conference? Please… Please… Please….'

'Oh, please allow me to finish. Leena, I will be unable to make it this year. Please, excuse me this time. I have some commitments which I cannot spell right now to you. But, do know that it must be something very important or else I would have surely come.'

There was a heavy pause that lingered on… I was disheartened with this bit of news.

Chirag went on, 'Hey, are you there? Or, have you dozed off?'

I replied in a dispirited voice, 'Is your work really very important? What if you finish attending to your commitments by then? The conference is two months away.'

'I know, and trust me, I would have loved to come and participate in it. And of course, it would have been lovely to meet you. Please, do not sound so despondent. Best wishes to you, and I know you will shine!'

I reverted to my tasks and immersed myself thoroughly in them and decided to not much think of Chirag's absence. *He was going to be missed not only by me, for he had become my mentor in all that I did or thought but his academic and technological prowess could have added to the quality of the conference. He was going to be missed by the students and other attendees too,* I knew.

Over the weekend, I was tempted to call him up again and try and persuade him to make it. Then I thought: *It has probably got something to do with his personal life. Perhaps, his wife will not let him come or they must be planning a family vacation?* I did not call him but he kept messaging me every other day, enquiring about the preparations and trying to cheer me up. I was confused too. *Why am I so much affected by whether he is coming or not? He is just a friend and it would have been nice to talk with him for a few days. Let me not make such a big deal out of the whole thing.*

Mom had been a staunch pillar of support in all these days—taking care of a lot of my e-mailing and filing work, getting printouts and even supervising my food and sleep. She vehemently insisted on me taking 4-5 hours off, on the Sunday before the conference commenced, and dragged me to a spa-and-salon and instructed them to rejuvenate me thoroughly—from head to toe.

This year, the conference spanned over four days. It began well, and the arrangements met everyone's expectations. There were many a new faces this year, from the academic as well as the corporate circuits. My days and nights were soaked in attending to all kinds of details and even to the inevitable shortcomings. The team of students which was assisting me was every bit as anxious as I was and every one of them was running around, trying to smooth out all the wrinkles as and when they surfaced.

During the post-lunch session on the third day, as I sat sipping a cup of tea in the networking lounge outside, someone tapped me on the shoulder. I turned around, and looked up. I was stunned.

Chirag stood there, smiling amiably with a look of mischief in his eyes.

I forgot that I was seated in the college with students all around. I leapt and hugged him, shrieking with joy all the while.

'Oh! I can't believe it... Are you really here? What a joyous surprise you have given me. How? All of a sudden? Howwwww? Whennnnn?'

He patted me on the head, and signalled me to take a seat. However, it was difficult for me to contain the euphoria. He was glad too, but calm and composed.

'So, Convener Madam, how are you? And how is the conference progressing?'

'But you... You had said that you cannot come this year,' I was still not myself.

'May I sit here?' he asked, politely.

I felt ashamed that I had not extended that courtesy all this time. 'Oh, I am sorry. Please, take a seat. Will you have tea or something cold, please?'

'Tea will be fine.' He was broadly grinning, and I could sense that he was amused at my flabbergasted reaction to his coming.

I beckoned one of the students to get a cup of tea along with some cookies and sandwiches. 'Yes, now you must tell me. How come you are here? Shall I arrange for you to make a presentation tomorrow? Oh, the students will love it!'

'It is such a pleasure to see you again after a year. It was certain that I was not going to be able to make it but things took such a turn that I had to come over. But please, do not arrange for any special lecture. I am not prepared and would never want to disturb the schedule. I am here for a week. You complete the tasks and we can meet whenever you are a little relaxed and free.'

'Oh, that is sad. Errr… I mean, it is great that you will be here for a week, but it is sad that you will not address the students this year. Okay, fine… I will be free by evening tomorrow and day after tomorrow will surely be declared a holiday by the Principal. Let's then meet the day after… Why don't you come home for lunch? Mom has been eager to meet you… She had instructed me to bring you home if you came for the conference.'

'Leena, can we meet at your place later? Would first like to have a long chat with you... If you are fine with it? Let's lunch at Punjab Grill on Friday?'

'Okay, done.' I was beaming now.

'Before I leave, I once again congratulate you, Leena. I am very proud of you. This conference is creating a buzz and the credit goes to you. If I had not come here personally and seen it all, you would not have told me how successful it was and the important role you played in its success. Keep going... See you, then.'

He left soon thereafter, while I sat bemused—staring at nothing. It was as if his praise had made it all worthwhile, as if that is what mattered to me the most.

The conference concluded with a roaring round of applause and I felt a mild thrill of success and achievement running down my veins. Of course, deep down I was aware that it was a team effort and that it could have been as successful even with someone else at the helm of affairs. This realisation kept me grounded.

I reached home late that night and thankfully remembered to tell Mom that I was going to be lunching with Chirag, the next day. Mom reiterated that I must finalise the plan for the next meal at our place. I hurriedly nodded and rushed to my room to catch up some good sleep.

Chirag was already seated in the restaurant when I reached. We were delighted to see each other, and after exchanging the initial pleasantries a bit courteously—the chattering was animated and mutual. There was quite a lot to ask and to know and to share and to listen. We (though, largely I) were making too many sounds of whoop and cheer; exclamations and shrieks that those around us frequently turned to stare at us. We were unmindful to that and continued....

After placing the order for a full three-course meal, Chirag turned and looked into my eyes. It felt strange and before I could open my mouth, he said, 'Leena, I want you to listen to me in total silence for the next ten minutes. There are a few details about my personal life I would like to share with you today.'

I was all ears... There were too many assumptions I had been making all this while about his personal life.

'Leena, I married a girl of my choice five years ago. She was and is a very fine person, but over the years, we drifted apart owing to our different perspectives. For instance, I began to become more philosophical and spiritual, and she was attracted to glitz and glamour. We both realised that not only were we moving in opposite directions, but we had also begun to pull the other in our own direction, on our individual path. A year ago, we decided to separate and we completed the formalities very amicably.'

I was breathing heavily, and my heart was not just beating normally; it was galloping.

Did they have kids? How many? Is he going to remarry? There were several questions I wanted to ask him, but he had told me to be silent till he completed what he had to say.

'In this one year, I have introspected much and tried to think clearly on what I wanted to do and the kind of decisions I felt I ought to take. Leena, I have decided to move back to India. My parents need me and I feel now is the most opportune time to return home. The prospects of our economy look quite promising.'

'Wow, splendid!' I cried out and many more necks turned towards me. I was so happy that tears welled up in my eyes. I felt as if my very own strong pillar of support was going to be near to me, from now onwards... I was ecstatic.

'Leena, listen to me carefully... I have loved our "we" moments and every bit of our talks and exchanges—whether over phone or email. I have been strongly drawn towards you, and though I know that you have been searching for the perfect groom for yourself, do I have a chance? Leena, will you consider me too? Do you think we can marry each other and that we could live happily married?'

I was stupefied; knocked out.

I could faintly hear Chirag calling out to me, but I was in a trance. It was a while before I felt a stirring in my heart, and a voice escaped my lips, 'Yesssssss!'

I blushed and got up to hug him... For several moments, I hugged him hard even as tears were streaming down my cheeks.

'Now, now...if you are going to cry like a baby and keep holding me, how will this "Unnamed Guy" bend on his knee and slip the ring on your finger while saying the three magical words?'

Unnamed Guy? I stared at him wide-eyed and dumbfounded.

The next instant, we both burst out laughing and the peals were the loudest this time....

The Last Word

'Also, Leena, before we make new beginnings, I want to tell you another thing. A few months ago, I was volunteering at a public school on a project for the restoration of their basketball court. It was something that a dear friend had asked for and I couldn't resist the opportunity to do some good for the community. During the stint of volunteering at the school, our team comprising ten of us—all volunteers, eking time from work and giving a few hours to the project, bonded well as a team. There was this one particular volunteer… Her name was Tara Jain.'

I looked up with a start. 'What did you say? Tara Jain?'

'Yes, Tara Jain. Why do you have this look? Do you know her?'

I lied sheepishly: 'No, I don't know her. It's just that the name sounded familiar. Don't bother. So, what happened to her?'

'No, nothing happened to her or to me, but yes, there was a kind of a spark. It could have turned out to be something genial but….'

'But…?'

Chirag looked at me transfixed and then gave out a short laugh. 'Oh God, you knew about this, isn't it? But how? Where? Okay, please… No need for you to be envious. It was nothing. Just a few fleeting moments of fascination which we both quickly realised were nothing but formal and professional regard for each other.'

I nodded. How badly I wanted to hide that relief sweeping all over my face! *Ought I to feel guilty or even confess about my stalking her online, twice…? Na, let it be,* I exonerated myself.

Chirag continued to look at me intently. He slowly smiled and said, 'Do you know that that brief episode with Tara during volunteering woke me from my slumber as far as you are concerned. It cleared the mist and I knew it is *you*, I want to spend life with.'

I sat there beaming.

I walked on cloud nine all the way home and flung myself into Mom's arms and hugged her rapturously!

'Oh Mom! Mom! My dear, dear Mom! You can never guess what happened today. You will be shocked. You will not believe it! You better sit down.'

Breathless and full of euphoria as I was, I gently led her to the sofa.

Mom turned around, and swung me towards the chair. 'Oh ho, Binnie… YOU are going to be in for a shock. I know the reason behind this joy that I see on my darling daughter's face. Who do you think guided Chirag at every step?' and she broke into fits of laughter.

'BAZINGA!' she exclaimed with a prize-winning expression on her face.

I was stunned.

The next minute, Mom held my face in her palms and murmured, 'Live happily, dear…always.'

'Mommmmmmmm, you knew it all? How? When? How, Mom?' I stumbled and bumbled in confusion.

She winked at me, held her stomach and another bout of uncontrollable laughter followed. Finally, she caught my arm and in a solemn conspiratorial tone whispered, 'Forget the whys and hows… Just give me all the details; an entire account of your romantic evening. Since five days I have been excitedly waiting to hear the details of this evening.'

'However, when did he take you into confidence? I mean, from which stage of his plan?'

'Oh ho…you leave all of that… Just tell me how did he propose to you?'

I knew I had no choice.

Having heard it all, she finally looked up and murmured a prayer.

'Jai ho! Jai ho! It is all due to the *matka* magic, dear! *Jai ho, Jai ho!'*

'What are you saying, Mom?'

'Don't you get it dear? It is all because of it! You must thank your second husband technically…errr, *Matkaji* for having blessed you with such a fine match! Let us go to Rishikesh one more time, and donate a hundred *matkas*. What say, Binnie?'

I sat transfixed on the sofa.

About the Authors

Navniit and Varuna are good friends, and though based in Kuwait and Gurugram (India) respectively, their sense of comic connects them and their expressions. While Navniit has written and published much by way of more than 250 feature articles and seven books, Varuna blogs on topics of health and fitness, and aspires to take this debut kick-off forward and write more.

Know more about Varuna here:

https://www.facebook.com/varunakhullar27
https://www.instagram.com/varuna927
https://twitter.com/yogawithv

Talk to Us

Dear Readers,

Were you reminded of a Leena or her Mom in your neighbourhood or family? We would love to read about your similar chuckling encounters and even your feedback on the book.

Write to us at: authors@shaadi-ka-laddoo.com

Visit us at: www.shaadi-ka-laddoo.com

Pip-pip...

Navniit and Varuna